Fairy Door

By

V. A. Boston

Copyright © 2020 by V. A. Boston

Cover © by BetiBup33_5666 on thecoverdesigner.com

All rights reserved. This book or any portion thereof may not be reproduced or used in any manner whatsoever without the express written permission of the publisher except for the use of brief quotations in a book review or scholarly journal. All person depicted herein are fictitious. Any resemblance to any person, living or dead, is purely coincidental.

ISBN 978-1-7342521-0-1

Botulf's Stone Press
www.bostonteatable.com

Fairy Door

To my parents, who always encouraged my writing, and to my fellow students who made it through this story's first draft. Thank you for your honest feedback and your encouragement!

Contents

Chapter 1 1

Chapter 2 17

Chapter 3 25

Chapter 4 35

Chapter 5 62

Chapter 6 86

Chapter 7 116

Chapter 8 125

Chapter 9 157

Chapter 10 174

Chapter 11 200

Chapter 12 216

Chapter 13 238

Chapter 14 253

Chapter 1

Midmorning sunlight, tinted with the heat of early summer, cast shadows between hills made green from the work of a storm-filled spring as Eibhlin made her way to the nearby town. Wind passed through her hair and danced between flowers that poked through the grass like drops of dye on a rumpled, green rug.

Eibhlin herself lived in a cottage along the eastern edge of the hills, built there by her great-grandfather before famine drove her grandparents from that home, and before her father brought her mother away from the gray mountains in the north back to that green-clothed country and its little town. The same little town where, three months ago, a thunderbolt had set thatched roofs to fire. No one died, but trades and treasures were lost, and many gained scars. Even the church now wore black on its stones, though otherwise it had been spared.

Her father had left early that morning to join the repair crews as he did every day, so he probably hadn't eaten. When she woke to her father's absence, Eibhlin had quickly tended to the chickens, packed a bag with biscuits and fresh boiled eggs, and left the house. She would have reached the town already had she used the path, but Eibhlin loved the rustle of grass and the rise and fall of earth beneath her feet. The dirt path curved around the hills before breaking two ways, one to the forestlands spreading up toward the Great Northern Mountains and out to the distant east, and the other path to the west where the White Cliffs loomed over ocean waves before swooping down to port towns and coastal villages. Eibhlin's goal, however, was the tiny town nestled between the hills and the forest.

Filled with no more than thirty families, it was more a village than a town and did not have a name. Most who passed through called it "the border town," as it lay near the river Lúrin that ran through the forest—the border of that country of Enbár—as well as near the White Cliffs, the border of the land itself. To the locals, it was one more border, that of between the hills rolling south to the lowland settlements and cities and the forest.

Townsmen called the woods magic, frequented by the fairy folk. Stories flew around of hearing fairy laughter or seeing dancing figures from the Fae Country between the trees. Some spoke of fairy help while others spoke of curses. Eibhlin believed every story. From the hilltop, she looked to the trees forming a line between land and sky, but a voice from below brought her back.

"Eibhlin, good morning!" called the voice. It belonged to an older man standing on the path with a bulging bag hanging from his shoulder.

"Good morning, Dr. Brien," said Eibhlin as she left the hill to join him. "How's the weavers'?"

"Nearly done," said the doctor. "Just the roof and the door and a few things left. Then it's on to the next one."

"Do you think they'll finish today?" she said.

"Probably not," he said. "But even if they do, I'm not sure what to do about the weavers' tools. Just about everything burned. The big caravans won't be through for a few months, but even when they do come, they won't have much to offer them. And it's not just the weavers'. Even if everyone pools their resources, we'll still have to hope things don't get too tight before next spring."

Eibhlin nodded in understanding.

As they came into town, folk greeted them from doorways. Eibhlin gave quick replies to each knowing nod at her satchel. They came into the main square where every available man carried, chopped, sawed, tied, or nailed lumber or did anything he could to keep busy. Women slipped between the chaos, children at their heels or infants slung across their backs as they filled whatever role they could.

One woman turned and saw Eibhlin and the doctor

approaching. "Welcome back, Brien," she said. "Did you find much? And good morning, Eibhlin."

"I had to go farther south than I'd expected and had to use the road on the way back, but I found enough herbs for today," said the doctor. "How are things here, Leana?"

"And have you seen my father?" added Eibhlin.

"There've been so many accidents already today, I might need to run back to the house for more thread," said Leana, looking through her husband's bag. "As soon as one injury is fixed, another two pop up. And your father is over there, helping thatch the weavers' house."

The once de-fleshed house was near healed. All around, men, women, and children bundled the dried reed into thatching and prepared the wooden spars used to bind it all together. One group of men lifted rough-cut beams to a pair standing on the walls where the roof would eventually be. Eibhlin called up to the pair balanced on the newly built walls. "Papa!"

Work stopped, and one of the men turned. He was a large man with a face bearing a full beard and bright, green eyes. Kind, lively eyes on a beast's body, that was Lochlann, blacksmith of the border town.

"Oi, Eibhlin!" came the voice of the other roof man. "What's your business this mornin'? The usual?"

Eibhlin held up her bag. The man laughed and

turned only to find himself alone on the incomplete building. When he looked back down to the ground, he couldn't see Eibhlin through Lochlann's broad back.

"Good morning, Eve-my-lin!"

"Good morning, Papa. I woke up late, so breakfast is a bit light," she said.

Lochlann laughed. "You don't need to be troubled about this old man."

"And you need to not trouble our neighbors," said Eibhlin. "They already make you lunch every day. I don't want them having to make you breakfast, too, or risk you falling over again from hunger."

One of the bundling men said, "Give it up, Lochlann. She's Kyra's daughter."

Lochlann's face softened to an expression Eibhlin knew well. Only one name made him make it. "You really are. I wish you could have known her better, Eve."

Eibhlin said, "I'm fine, Papa. No, really, I am. I hardly even remember Mama, anyway."

Lochlann smiled, though slightly, and lifted the satchel from his daughter's shoulder. "Sorry to make you bring this again."

"If it bothers you," said the wall-top man, "why don't you sleep in, eat breakfast at home for a change."

"How can you say that when there's still so much work to do?" said Lochlann.

"How indeed," said Eibhlin. "Please don't worry

about me. I don't mind the walk, and it's good to get out of the house, anyway."

From beside an injured worker, Brien said, "Maybe you don't mind, but your father needs more rest. Skipping meals, working long, hard days, you'll make yourself sick at this rate, Lochlann."

"Oh, Doctor, you're back," said Lochlann. "How's the morning so far?"

"Not as bad as yesterday, he said, unrolling a strip of bandage cloth, "but still too many workers rushing to finish jobs, making mine that much busier."

"And you're telling me to rest more when you're busy yourself?" said Lochlann.

"I'm a doctor," said Brien. "It's my job to not rest so my patients can, and I don't need you on that list, too."

"I say you both need rest," said Leana. "Really, it's like you two are trying to work yourselves to death."

Eibhlin spoke. "It's fine. Maybe Papa works too much, but if his body really needs to rest, it'll tell him. Besides, he's working to help everyone. Isn't that a good thing?"

Doctor Brien said nothing, but his wife sighed. She said, "You have a good daughter, Lochlann. Make sure you take care of her properly."

"But of course! Don't you trust me?" he said.

"It's not quite that," she said. Leana glanced to her

husband, but his eyes stayed focused on the wrapping bandage. She said to Eibhlin, "If you ever need help, just tell me, okay?"

"Oh, I'm fine," said Eibhlin. "Don't worry about me and just focus on getting everyone else fixed up."

Leana frowned but said nothing more.

"By the way, do you need me as an extra hand?" asked Eibhlin.

Doctor Brien answered, "Actually, yes, that would be great. Almost everyone not working on houses is out with the flocks, so if you could help a bit, we'd appreciate it."

"Okay," said Eibhlin. "Papa, don't forget to eat your breakfast. Also, tonight I'll have potato and chicken soup for dinner, so don't come back too late, or it'll be cold."

Lochlann beamed. "I guess I'll need to be home early, then."

Before Eibhlin could say anything more, a crash came from down the road, and she and the doctors rushed off. From there, the morning passed quickly as Eibhlin ran around town patching up one injury after another. As the noon bell tolled, she sat with Leana eating a light lunch of biscuits and cheese while Brien met with the men to discuss the afternoon's tasks.

"Do you really need to head back?" asked Leana.

Eibhlin nodded. "I need to check the garden, and

then there's cleaning to do and dinner to make and whatever else might pop up. I don't want to risk going late."

"Yes, that's true," said Leana. "Things usually take more time than you think. You know, you don't have to worry about dinner. Brien and I could- Oh! Could it be today is—"

"Yeah. It's Papa's birthday," said Eibhlin, dropping her voice. "But don't remind anyone. They'll want to stop working to celebrate, and what kind of gift would that be to that man?"

The two finished their lunch in silence, but as Eibhlin prepared to leave, Leana said, "Your father is lucky to have a daughter like you."

Eibhlin blushed. "No, he isn't. Not at all!"

"No, Eve, he is," said Leana. "Between you and your mother, he's been very lucky.... Listen, Eibhlin, don't be too generous with your father, and if you need help, please let us know. Any time."

The blush grew. "I understand," said Eibhlin as she made her way to the hills.

When she crossed her own threshold, Eibhlin slumped against the door, letting herself slide to the floor.

"She's a good daughter." "Your father is lucky."

A scoff slipped from her throat.

She looked around the room, a list sounding off in

her head like parts of a creed. In one wall sat the fireplace, its stones black with soot and pit full of ash. And nearby stood the splinter-topped table, a single chair beside it. Another chair lay against the wall by the fireplace, one leg stacked with the wood. The sheet nailed across the shutter-less window flew loose from a gust of wind. A whistle snuck between cracks in the old roof, and dust sat everywhere. The chickens ran defenseless, the coop door gone, and two hens lost last week. Weeds overgrew the garden. The list ever lengthened. Eibhlin forced herself up. She hurried from task to task, thinking how her father would return soon. This time. This time, he would come back.

Evening came. Over the fire bubbled a pot of soup. Between facing sets of tableware sat a small jar of jam and leftover biscuits from lunch. Eibhlin pulled over the kitchenware chest as a makeshift bench and fell across it with a deep exhale. Outside, a growl of thunder threatened rain as moist wind pushed against and slipped through the window-sheet. Eibhlin smiled. If it stormed, construction would stop. No torchlight work. He would surely be home soon.

The first drops of rain struck against the roof. Time passed, and still she sat alone. But this was expected. Preparing the building sites for the storm and walking the road back home would take time, especially in the dark and rain. This delay couldn't be helped. Soon, though, her father would burst through the door, perhaps soaked, and go to the bedroom to change. They would hang his clothes by the fire to dry, and he would have stories, of course, of the workers' sudden rush to defend their sites and of the great works of men's combined strength.

As Eibhlin thought this, the raindrops turned to sheets, and she clenched her sleeves.

The rain fell harder and harder. More than once, Eibhlin jumped up from her makeshift bench to pull out a pot for a new leak. By the time the rain slowed, she had used every spare pot, bowl, and cup, and the only thing to have burst open was the window-sheet, sending her near into panic as she struggled to put it back and stop the water pooling beneath her.

Wet hair stuck to her face as the girl shrank by the fire into a blanket's folds. She looked to the door. Perhaps the sudden storm had kept him in town. Or had something happened to him? No, someone would have told her. Unless they didn't know yet. She pulled the blanket over her head, stretched her cold toes toward the fire, and decided that clean up must have simply taken too long and her father was now waiting out the rain. Soon. Very soon. Just a little longer.

The rain passed.

Minutes slid away, then hours. Pain settled in her stomach. She removed the pot from the fire to keep the broth from boiling out and watched the steam gradually vanish. Water dripping through the roof reflected the light like drops of fire. Not one thump of boots. Not one creak of hinges. Just the sounds of crackling wood, drips of fire, and a hungry stomach. But not for long. Soon. Just a little longer. A little long—

"Aaaaaargh!"

Eibhlin slammed her fist against the floor. She rose, took the broken chair, and struck it against the fireplace. Splinters sprayed across the floor and into the soup as she dashed wood against stone. She tossed the headrest into the fire and stomped to the bedroom.

Heading to her father's side, she turned out the trunk sitting at the foot of his bed. She tore the blanket from the bed, and with the last of her strength, she took the pillow and pounded it against walls, beds, and floor till it burst. She sank to the floor, burying her face in the pillow's remains, goose feathers falling like downy rain.

Again! He had forgotten her again! He said he would be back. He had... he had....

Eibhlin lifted her face. Seeing the room, all evidence of that day's cleaning gone, she felt a fresh set of tears forming and moved her gaze to the blanket on the floor, as if thinking to hide beneath it. Then she saw it, half-buried beneath the crumpled pile of clothes and blanket. She pulled the blanket up.

It was a small smithy hammer. Her father being a blacksmith, she wouldn't have found it too strange to keep a spare hammer among his things but for the hammer's appearance. It was forged of silver from head to handle's end. Set into the pommel was an icy blue stone held in place by jagged, silver tendrils and two reptilian tails. The tails melted into the naked handle, crossing as they wound up to the head, where each joined a dragon's body. From the dragons' mouths, lighting shot toward the hammer's face.

Taking up the item, Eibhlin thought how light it felt despite its material. Familiarity flittered across her mind. She had seen this hammer before, but she couldn't remember when. Running her fingers across the dragon heads, she said, "It's beautiful, but what good is a hammer made of silver?"

"None, it seems, to you, if it was stored in such a manner."

Eibhlin stiffened and turned to the voice. Standing on a bedpost was a tiny woman. Black hair spread behind her like a cloak, causing her pale body to appear nearly white. Large, dark eyes locked onto Eibhlin as transparent wings twitched against the fairy's back. Flying from the bedpost to the hammer, she reached out and brushed long, thin fingers against the silver. "Amazing work," she said. "More so than I remembered. Human child, will you sell to me this hammer?"

"You... you're a fairy!" said Eibhlin.

"Yes, and you are a human," said the fairy without a change in tone. "Now, will you sell me the hammer?"

"I thought fairies rarely approached humans."

"Rarely, but not never. Now, the hammer—"

"The-the hammer? What about it?" asked Eibhlin.

"I wish to buy it from you," said the fairy. "Of course, the price is yours to set."

Eibhlin held the hammer closer. "Why do you want this? You can't forge anything with a hammer made of a soft metal like silver. It's useless."

"To humans, yes. To humans, it is no more than a decoration," said the fairy.

"But not to you?" asked Eibhlin.

"It is useful to all but human kind," said the fairy. "This hammer crafts with magic. It's a powerful tool, elven made and ancient, and none alive are skilled enough to make another like it. In proper hands, it has shattered diamonds, among its baser actions. But in human hands, invoking its enchantments overwhelms the user and often leads to death. Such is the nature of great and ancient magic."

Eibhlin caught her breath. She stared at the hammer, turning it over in her hand and in her mind. With a quiet voice, she said, "And you want me to sell you something so incredible?"

"Have you a reason to refuse me?" said the fairy.

Eibhlin did. Clearly her father valued this thing if he kept it despite being unable to use it, and if he hadn't sold it by now, he probably didn't plan to. However, he had also left her to handle the house and finances on her own, and when the merchant trains came, she would need something to trade for necessities. With how little the forge's fire had been lit recently, or would be in the coming weeks, there wouldn't be many options.

"What's your offer?" she asked. "You more or less said this thing is priceless. How can you match that?"

With a clap louder than Eibhlin would expect from hands so small, the fairy grew to nearly her father's height. From a pocket on her belt, the fairy removed a small, leather pouch. She reached in and pulled out a polished gold coin. The fairy held out the coin. "Take it and test it however you wish."

Eibhlin let the heavy metal press against her palm. It caught the light from the fire in the next room, giving the circle a shining rim. Eibhlin swallowed the tremble in her voice. "So... you'll give me some gold coins? How does that even come close to 'priceless'?"

"A king's coffers could not meet the hammer's value," said the fairy. "However, this is but a sample. Your hand, please."

Eibhlin held out her hand, and the fairy tipped the

purse. A stream of gold poured out, drowning Eibhlin's lap and the floor in an outspreading flood of coins. Only when the fairy righted the purse did the flow of money stop. With coins slipping through her fingers, Eibhlin said, "How did you—where did they come from?"

The fae creature said, "This purse opens to my treasury. I possess greater wealth than any mortal king could gather over lifetimes, but I have no use for it. It would be yours to spend. The closest one could come to 'priceless,' yes? Have we a deal?"

Eibhlin weighed the hammer in one hand and the gold in the other. The hammer was probably important to her father, but the house needed repair. And all the work must be done by a lone girl as she also cooked, cleaned, and brought things to her father and helped the town. Brien told her as much that morning. Not a free hand could be spared, and certainly not her father's. Merchants were not charities, and there was simply too much to prepare.

But if she sold the hammer? Could she not ease the town's worry? Would that not free up some hands to help her? Perhaps even her father's? What was a decoration to a safe, warm house and everyone's livelihoods? Her father was never home to use or even look at it anyway.

Eibhlin held out the hammer. "Deal."

A flash of emotion briefly filled the fairy's face. Gently, she took the hammer and replaced it with the purse and said, "Our transaction is finished. Fare you well, human child. Doing business was a pleasure."

With that, the fairy shrank and shot off into the dark, leaving Eibhlin alone and clutching her new wealth.

Chapter 2

Fear filled Eibhlin when the door finally opened.

Soon after trading the hammer, weariness had sent her to bed, but when she woke that morning to everyday sounds and a sunlit house, dread invaded her mind. She knew that when her father returned she would need to tell him what she had done. Hiding a bag of infinite gold couldn't last long. How to tell him, though, that was hard. As she cleaned the previous night's wreckage and returned the spilt gold to the purse, she formed and reformed her explanation, but no matter how she reasoned it, something pricked at her mind. When her father entered that afternoon, a broad smile on his face, a chill settled in her chest and fingertips.

"Good day, Eibhlin, dear!" said Lochlann, kissing her forehead. "You weren't worried last night, I hope."

"Good afternoon, Papa," she managed.

Her father went on. "Whew! I tell you, Eve, that rain yesterday nearly got us. We were in the middle of putting down the thatch, three men on each side, when we suddenly started hearing thunder. I don't think I've seen men work so hard or so fast these past months to get that thatching and everything under cover. The wonders of men's combined strength. That's what it was. And you know, Eve, we did it. Just barely made it, but we did. Then the rain came, and by the time we got to the pub to celebrate, we were soaked. I was so cold and wet, I must have spent an hour by the fire. But we beat the rain. Ha!"

"Um... Papa, um... there's something I need to—"

"And then this morning, we got up and went straight to work, and now the weavers' roof is half done! You should've seen everyone's faces. And then- oh! What am I doing? I got mud all over the floor. Sorry about that. I just came to check on you and to grab a quick change of clothes, but I'll clean that up before I head back."

As her father approached the bedroom, Eibhlin said, "Papa, I have something I need to—"

"Just a moment, Eibhlin. I'll be right out."

"Oh... okay," said Eibhlin. She watched the door groan shut.

From the room, she heard the chest hinges creak. Less than a minute later, Lochlann nearly tripped out of the room, his face tight. He opened the dish chest and looked in every pot and under every mouse-nibbled blanket. After a couple minutes of watching his frantic search, Eibhlin asked, "What is it, Papa?"

"You probably wouldn't know it," said Lochlann,

motioning with his hands even as his eyes continued searching around the room, "but I have a thing, a silver hammer. Usually, I keep it buried in my trunk, but I can't find it. I can't find it, Eve! It's gone. I don't know where—"

"I know about it," said Eibhlin.

"Really?" said Lochlann. "It's been years, hasn't it, since I last showed it to you? Before your mother, well, but I suppose you could remember it, couldn't you? No, I shouldn't be surprised. Have you seen it recently? I mean, since a couple days ago? I can't—"

"I sold it."

Lochlann stared at his daughter. "You... what? What? I-I don't...."

Struggling to keep her voice level, Eibhlin said, "I sold the hammer, Father. I found it last night and sold it."

"You... do you know what you've done?" said Lochlann, his voice tightening with each word.

Eibhlin held up the purse. "I didn't sell it for nothing. Look. Gold comes out. It's magic. We can even use it to help everyone in town. Isn't it amazing? Besides, isn't this much more useful than some wall decoration?"

"Décor... You thought the hammer was...." Lochlann collapsed into the chair.

"Papa?"

The man didn't shout, but Eibhlin felt his words weigh down her stomach like wet sand in a sack. "That hammer, that 'decoration,' was your mother's," he said. "It was a gift from your grandfather, a family heirloom. It was the only thing besides the clothes on her back that she brought with her, the only connection she had to her family, and the only thing of hers left to me when she died. And you sold it? How could you do that? Now, the last thing I had left of hers is gone! And all because you wanted money?"

Heat burst to Eibhlin's face.

Grabbing the purse from her, Lochlann slammed it onto the table. "All for money. You sold your mother's heirloom, and all for this bag and some gold coins!"

"I didn't know," she said.

"What?" said Lochlann.

"I. Didn't. Know," she said. "I didn't know it was Mama's, and how could I? You never told me. You never tell me anything about her. What she looked like. What kind of person she was. Nothing. Ever. You never talk about anything besides your work. That's everything to you, isn't it? Why should you care about some hammer? You don't care about anything besides working."

"Now hold on, Eibhlin, you know that's not true," Lochlann said, his voice bordering on disbelief at the accusation.

Eibhlin scoffed. "Isn't it? Ha! That's right. It's not about work. Then you might actually show some care for our home. No. It's all about helping someone else. It's all about working for nothing while your own house falls apart. I can't fix this place by myself, but you're always too busy helping someone else to bother helping me. Someone else is always more important to you. You leave your own house crumbling, but when it's someone else's, you'll do whatever it takes, even race a storm."

"Eibhlin—"

"And then there're your 'promises'," said Eibhlin, feeling her stomach knot as she spoke but driven onward by the anger heating her cheeks. "They're a joke! Just once, couldn't you actually mean it?"

"Eibhlin, I'm not a liar. You know I'm a man of my word," he said.

"For other people!" Eibhlin screamed. "Yesterday, your birthday, you said you'd be back early, and like an idiot, I believed you. Really, I'm such an idiot. But, no, never again. I'm never going to fall for it again. I know that compared to anyone and anything else, I don't matter to you. No matter what I do, I'm just your daughter. Well I wish I wasn't. That way, you'd treat me just like everyone else. I wish I had never been born your daughter!"

"That's enough!" said Lochlann, rising from the

chair with such force that he knocked over the table, gold coins pouring from the magic purse. Eibhlin's mouth clamped shut as control over her tears broke and they ran down her face as he stared at her, his face flushed and eyes flashing with anger. However, on seeing the tears, Lochlann's voice became choked as he reached out to touch her wet cheeks. "Eibhlin, Eve, I... I didn't—"

"Don't touch me," the girl cried, jerking back. Before the man could protest, Eibhlin turned and ran out the door, slamming it shut to mask the sound of her father calling after her.

On and on she ran, the work of her body pushing the sobs back into her throat. Up, down, over, and around smooth hills till they turned to rocky masses topped with grass. Slowly, the hills diminished until only grass and rock remained. Over the sound of her pounding feet rose the sound of pounding waves, and the smell of salt water filled the growing wind.

At last, she could see the end: the border of the country, the border of the earth itself, the White Cliffs. Nearing the edge, she slowed, but only enough to more carefully descend along the natural path covered in pebbles and puddles of last night's rain. Down, down she went until she reached a small outcrop of rock and sea salt, and there, with burning lungs and aching legs, she fell to the ground.

Thunderous roaring rent the air as the ocean lay siege upon the cliff sides. All sound gave way to the boom and echo of wave against rock. Within the safety of the crash of waves and the quaking air, with her pale hair the color of cold sunlight lashing her face, she cried.

She cried till the sky darkened, cried till her head hurt, cried till it was too painful to cry. And as the cries left her body, her mind, too, screamed, questions pounding her spirit like the waves did the cliffs. Why? She had never seen her father so furious. Or so sad. Why had this happened? How had this happened? What was she supposed to do?

Eibhlin shivered in the wind and sea spray.

This was all because of that fairy! Because of that deal, everything had fallen apart. All because of trading away the hammer. Staring out at the sea, Eibhlin whispered, "Well, then, I'll just have to get it back."

Moonlight mothered shadows as Eibhlin slid through the doorway. She could make out her father's shape, his head cushioned on his arms as he slept at the righted table. On the wood surface, catching hints of cold light from the doorway, glinted the gold coins sitting around their enchanted purse. Wincing with every creak of the floor, Eibhlin grabbed her satchel, hastily tiptoed into the bedroom, and changed into a clean dress. She grabbed the remaining clothes from her trunk, along with a bronze knife, and stuffed them into the bag. After putting on her cloak, she returned to and crept around the main room, grabbing some food, the jar of jam, a flask of water, and finally the fairy purse and its shimmering coins.

As she placed the purse in her satchel, she heard her father groan and froze. When she saw he remained asleep, she risked putting her hand on his curly head and whispered, "I'll be back. Don't worry. I'll fix everything.

With those parting words, she slipped out the door, closing it as silently as she could, and ran away, leaving behind the only place she had ever known.

Chapter 3

Little could be seen through the midnight shadows of the forest men called enchanted. She didn't have a light, so Eibhlin set herself beneath a large beech tree just beyond the tree line, hugged herself in her cloak, and after a few minutes fell asleep. When she woke, her body was stiff in the chill air. Sunlight passing through leaves tinted the world in soft green and gold.

After a few painful stretches, Eibhlin stood to her feet and took out a biscuit to eat while walking. She needed to find a fairy. Deeper into the forest she went. The ground foliage thickened, causing her to trip on hidden sticks, roots, branches, and stones. The thought already arose to abandon her search, but she clutched a gold coin and went deeper. Deer, rabbits, birds, insects, she saw plenty of wild life, but not a single sign of a fairy.

As afternoon arrived, she heard the sound of water and followed it to the wide river Lúrin, the border of Enbár, a river quickened from the recent rain. Eibhlin took off her shoes and stepped into the river, shivering as cold water bent around her ankles. She looked up through breaks in the trees to the bright sky. By now, her father was certainly awake and looking for her, or maybe even sending out a search party, and many in town knew the woods far better than she did. With that thought, she shook the numbness from her feet, dried them with her cloak, and slipped them back into her shoes. She mustn't be found, not yet.

She followed the river south. Leana had once said the river led down to the sea. "Might as well head that way," said Eibhlin. "At least it's somewhere."

It was about an hour down river that her luck turned. In the heat of the day, over the river's chatter, at first faint enough she thought it was her imagination, she heard singing. As she continued downstream, the voice grew clearer, as clear as cold starlight, and the words were not anything Eibhlin knew. Curiosity turned her from the river. Hope kept her quiet.

Not far into the undergrowth, she came to the voice's origin, and it was only her careful eye that kept her from stepping too far, for she saw a small fairy singing as she skipped around a near perfect ring of mushrooms. A fairy ring, a gateway into the Fae Country. Sweat chilled on the back of Eibhlin's neck. A fairy! What luck, and yet what terrible circumstances! One wrong move, and Eibhlin could fall through the fairy ring and find herself lost in the Fae Country. And then what? But time didn't favor her, and the fairy was there.

Creeping closer, Eibhlin took off her cloak and waited till the fairy hopped to the closest mushroom, and then the girl pounced, throwing her cloak over the tiny woman. If she had not surprised the fairy, Eibhlin might have died a cursed frog. As it was, she managed to capture the creature in the layers of cloth. The fairy nearly broke free, but Eibhlin curled over the bundle and pinned it to the forest floor. From inside the cloak came several shrieks and what sounded like half-formed curses.

"Calm down, Miss Fairy," shouted Eibhlin. "I don't want to hurt you. I just need to ask you something."

The fairy stopped. "Ask me something?"

"Yes. You see I—"

"I shall not answer anything so long as you treat me like a bug," said the fairy. "Next thing I know, you'll stick me in a jar and pull off my wings."

"Please! Just a few questions," said Eibhlin.

The fairy fell silent for a few moments then said, "Let me go. I won't speak with you while you hold me captive. Such inconsideration!"

Eibhlin relaxed and moved. The fairy shot from the cloak. Landing on a high tree branch, she began to laugh. "Silly, stupid human!" she said. "If you want to force a fairy's help, don't let it go so easily next time."

Eibhlin flushed to her ears. "Well, you're free. Now won't you answer my questions?"

The fairy started straightening her hair. "Not at all."

"What! Why?"

"Why should I help you?" said the fairy. "If you've got a problem, fix it yourself. Why do I need to get involved? There's nothing in it for me, anyway. So, since it's a nice day, I'll let you go, but try anything like that again and you'll wish I had drowned you in the Lúrin. Now, bye-bye."

As the fairy flew away, Eibhlin said, "Wait! Wait! Um... how... how about a deal!"

The fairy's ears twitched. Glancing down, she asked, "What kind of deal?"

"I give you something you want in exchange for answers to my questions. Simple as that," said Eibhlin.

For a long moment, the fairy hovered, staring at Eibhlin with a blank expression. Finally, the fairy said, "Sweets."

"Huh?"

"Sweets," the fairy said. "I smell sweets. If you give me the sweets you have in your bag, I'll answer three questions as best I can."

"Oh, okay." Eibhlin pulled out a biscuit and the jam from her bag. The little fairy grew to the height of a small child and snatched the treats. She dipped a slender finger into the jam and scooped some into her mouth before spreading sticky fruit preserves over the biscuit. Between nibbles, the fairy said, "All right, give me some context and ask your three questions."

After Eibhlin's summary, the fairy frowned. "A fairy from two days back. Long, black hair, dark but bright eyes, and a taste for enchanted artifacts? Sounds like you made a deal with the fairy your country calls Mealla."

"Then you know her!" said Eibhlin.

"I know about her, and it would be shameful if I didn't," said the fairy. "She's famous in the Fae Realm as someone not even royals mess with. Why would you do such a stupid thing as make a trade with Mealla? No matter how long I spend under the Mortal Sun, I still can't understand humans."

"I didn't know who she was," said Eibhlin. "Now, for my first question, I need to find this Mealla. Where and how can I find her?"

"That's actually two questions, but I'll let it slide this time," said the fairy, taking another lick of jam. "As for 'where' she is, I can't really tell you. See, a long time ago, even for us Fae, Mealla cast some potent protection spells around her home. It's possible to find it on accident, but to just go there? I don't think even the royal family could, not that they'd risk it. So, to just 'find' Mealla on purpose is impossible."

"That can't be!" said Eibhlin. "I have to—"

"Don't interrupt. So inconsiderate! Anyway, I can't

tell you 'where' Mealla is exactly, but I can tell you how to get there," said the fairy.

"But didn't you—You just said finding her on purpose is impossible," said Eibhlin.

The fairy huffed. "Interruptions. Interruptions. Do you want answers or not? As I was about to say, it's impossible unless you follow certain steps."

"Steps?" asked Eibhlin.

"Second question," said the fairy, to which Eibhlin mentally cursed herself. The fairy continued, "You need to use a certain fairy door that goes straight to her home, and for that you'll need three keys. Special fairy keys Mealla made. After making them, though, Mealla hid them in the Mortal Realm, and only she knows where they all are or where the door is. I do know where to look for one of the keys, though, if the rumors are true."

"Really? Where?' said Eibhlin.

"Far away, in a place too far to reach in a season on foot," said the fairy.

"Can't you be more specific?" cried Eibhlin. "And what am I supposed to do after that? Search the world for keys when I don't even know where to start?"

"Not my problem. I've already answered three questions. Our business is finished," the fairy said.

Eibhlin said, "Wait! Isn't there anything else you know? I'll trade for it. I have to find Mealla."

With a sidelong glance, the fairy sighed and said, "I've really spent too long here in the Mortal Realm. Fine. I'll do what I can. I mean, you *did* let me go instead of pulling my wings off, after all, so consider this my gratitude."

"Thank you!" said Eibhlin.

"I'm not doing much, just getting rid of you. Don't be so happy about it," said the fairy. "Come on. Let's get this over with."

River rock held back trees, forming a clearing, in the place where the fairy stopped. Standing alone near the edge of the Lúrin was a large, wide willow covered in knots. The fairy led Eibhlin to the riverside tree.

Eibhlin asked, "Why are we here?"

"More questions?" said the fairy. "This tree, silly human, is a fairy door. If you unlock it, you can go to wherever its road connects to."

"Unlock? How?"

Smirking, the fairy reached out her hand. Light twisted together to form the shape of a key that shone soft, white light. "This is what you humans call a 'fairy key.' It can open almost any door, magic or not. You'll be looking for similar keys, only since they're Mealla's, the ones you want are bound to specific doors. Now listen carefully. I'm going to open the fairy door in this tree. It's just an ordinary door to an ordinary fairy road, but I can use my magic to connect this road to another road I've heard leads to one of Mealla's keys. Oh, don't look so amazed. Connecting roads is nothing special. However, don't get comfortable. Our doors like to just go one way, so joined roads can be a little unstable. They only last a couple trips before the bond breaks and they go back to normal. After that, don't risk it. You don't know where you could end up. Understand?"

Eibhlin nodded. "Yes. Thank you."

With a return nod, the fairy approached the tree and slid the white key into a knot in the bark. She jerked it slightly counter clockwise then turned it the other way. *Click.* Rays of light burst from the keyhole like the sun behind an eclipse, but nothing else seemed to change. The fairy removed the key, and its light slipped away into the keyhole, leaving behind a simple, tarnished key.

"What happened?" Eibhlin asked.

"The key just lost its magic. Normal fairy keys are one use only. Mealla's keys are different. You'll see when you find them. There's no mistaking them, even by a human. Well, there's your road," said the fairy.

"My road," Eibhlin whispered. The light from the keyhole sent tingles up and down her spine. She shivered and stepped toward it.

"H-human!"

Eibhlin turned to the fairy.

"Gi-give me some of your hair. Nine strands. That should be enough," said the fairy.

"Why?" said Eibhlin.

"Just do it," the fairy said, her pale skin tinted pink.

Eibhlin plucked the requested number and handed over the long strands. Light gathered at the fairy's fingertips. With the hair held tight in one hand, she took the strands with the other and, faster than Eibhlin could see, wove them into a tiny braid. However, it was not a braid of hair but of pale gold. After joining the ends, the fairy handed the chain to Eibhlin, saying, "An apology, for laughing at you. Use this to hold the keys. The chain will never break or fall off your neck or leave you without your permission."

"But there's no clasp. How did you join it?" said Eibhlin as she took the chain.

"Must light have a clasp to join together?"

Eibhlin could only shake her head. "Thank you, Miss Fairy. Thank you very much."

Facing away, the fairy said, "I don't know why you're thanking me. Silly human! It's just a business deal, nothing more. Trying to catch me like a bug and then thanking me? Stupid! I'm not going to waste any more time here. I do have things to do, after all. You need to hurry, too. The door won't stay open for long."

The fairy took off, but as she shrank and flew away, she glanced back and said, "May Lady Fortune favor you, human."

Eibhlin waved as the fairy disappeared into the woods. Then, taking a deep breath and pulling the chain over her head, she stepped toward the fairy door.

Chapter 4

Eibhlin could never quite describe the experience of traveling through a fairy door. It left much in her mind, but no clear likeness through which to bring it from the sensational to the sensory. Like magic in the abstract. The most she could explain was feeling a slight pull. Beyond that, all sense memories sifted together, leaving behind only vague impressions she couldn't grasp or separate.

Then she found herself caged in darkness. At first, fear rose, and she threw out her arms to find any guide for her senses. Her hands touched smoothed wood. She pressed against the wood, and something creaked. Pushing a little harder, the wood swung outward, revealing a clean, barren room. On the far side of the room stood a dark wood door carved with leaves and vines along the edges and some sort of solar symbol in its center. Fully opening her own door, she started stepping through when the far door suddenly swung open. Standing in the threshold, practically hanging from the handle, was a young boy with dark hair, silver eyes, and pointed ears.

Eibhlin didn't know what to say. Here she was

coming through a stranger's door, and an interior door at that, judging from the room, in what was probably an elf's home, since elves rarely brought small children beyond their own borders. Feeling her stomach churn under the child's stare, Eibhlin said, "Hello, um... I went through a fairy door, and it led me here. I'm not trying to break in or anything. This is just where the road ended, you see, so, well, I'm sorry if I scared you."

In response, the child ran off, yelling in a language Eibhlin couldn't understand. Eibhlin groaned. She hadn't considered language barriers. Hopefully someone in the area understood fairy doors so she wouldn't need to try explaining her presence. As she stepped past her door, Eibhlin nearly fell as she found the floor farther down than expected. Turning, she saw she had just entered the room from the slightly raised door of a large wardrobe. She groaned again and hoped even more that someone here understood fairy doors.

The sound of approaching feet returned her attention to the far door. She saw the child again and behind him a lithe man that among humans might be in his early thirties, but his youthful appearance didn't match the age in his eyes. The adult elf entered the room, the child holding his hand. Stopping in front of her, he looked first toward Eibhlin and then toward the wardrobe. Eibhlin didn't know if she should speak when she didn't know if he could understand her.

Then, much to her relief, he said in her own language, "Elkir said a human of Enbár had come through Mealla's wardrobe, but it's still surprising. Would you mind explaining yourself, please?"

"You know Mealla?" said Eibhlin.

The elf smiled. "In a way, yes, though not usually by that name. It's a very human name."

"Is it? I heard it from the fairy that connected another fairy door to this one. I need to speak with Mealla, and she, the other fairy, said coming here is the first step."

"Did she?" said the elf, looking from Eibhlin to the wardrobe and back. "Well, I suppose further explanation can wait till we get you some rest and nourishment. Come, come. A trip through a fairy road is no light task, especially for a human. Follow me. By the way, Miss, what's your name?"

For a moment, Eibhlin's eyes met the elf's, and the glimpse of aged silver brought to mind stories saying elves can read through lies. Her muscles tensed, but she gave a simple, "I'm Eibhlin. And you are?"

Motioning to himself and then to the child, he said, "I am Chensil, and this is my son, Elkir. I'm the caretaker of Mealla's road in this settlement."

Down hall after hall they went, short stone tunnels leading to room after room. More than once, Eibhlin looked out thin windows and saw rows of windows much like their own or, sometimes, wide-trunked trees and undergrowth, but she and her guides did not stop for a more careful look. As halls crossed their own, Chensil turned corners with the confidence of familiarity. Eventually, they came to a wide room with a high, domed ceiling carved with leaves and waves transitioning to clouds and fire. Above those were the seven heavenly spheres circling skylights patterned after the fixed stars and their constellations. Eibhlin had just found the Western Leadstar when she and her guides left through decorated double doors into the outside.

They stood at the top of a small, stone stairway facing short houses with wooden roofs scattered across a flat prairie of tall grass and taller flowers. Unlike in a proper town, the grass had not been cleared to make way for the houses. Roads roughly cobbled with river stones cut through the grass from house to house, the knee-high grass resembling the stone walls that sometimes bordered roads back home, disrupted only where vanity paths wore down the grass. Alongside everything ran a broad, slow river, across which she saw nothing but prairie and sky. There was a subdued wildness to the combination of those scattered houses, the unkept and untilled ground, and the wide expanse of grass and sky, as if the community sat along some border as easily crossed as the grass walls to their roads. From their vantage point on the steps, Eibhlin saw several elves going about their business from house to house as children ran through the grass or splashed and fished in the river.

"Not much to look at, is it?"

Eibhlin turned to Chensil. "I think it's pretty, and I've never seen the sky look so big!"

"Well, we can't take credit for the sky, now can we?" he said. "But we like it here. It's open, where most of our brethren prefer enclosed spaces and trees that block the sky. Some of us, though, prefer to know the sun and moon and stars. We're a bit more like the Fae, in that way, than the Mortal Realm."

Before Eibhlin could ask his meaning, Chensil spoke to his son, and the boy released his father's hand and sped down the stairs. "Where's he going?" asked Eibhlin.

"To tell my wife and daughter of your coming," Chensil replied. "Guests should receive a proper welcome."

As they followed Elkir's path, Eibhlin looked back to see the building they had left, and her steps stopped. Beyond a low, white building stretching for what seemed like miles, trees towered, their branches twisting together so tightly Eibhlin could barely tell one from another. They bridged the river, creating a green-tinted tunnel from which the water came. And beyond even that, far in the distance, stood mountains whose tips hid behind clouds. Eibhlin's lungs felt too small for the air she needed, and she wondered how any could stand living between those encroaching giants and the overwhelmingly vast sky.

Chensil's voice interrupted her silent wonder. "The Hall was here before we came. Its enchantments hold the forest at bay, though what craft could hold back such trees is lost to us now. The river then comes down from the peaks of the Northern Mountains, through the forest, and into open space, making this a place where boundaries meet. That's probably why the Hall was built here, as a meeting place between the Mortal and the Fae."

Eibhlin nodded. For the next few minutes, she walked backwards, taking in more of the long building standing like a wall between the prairie and the forest. It was unadorned, with a simple roof and plaster walls, yet even with its short stature, as Eibhlin continued looking at it, she began to imagine it standing defiantly against the trees and the mountains, and she felt her breath come easier again.

Chensil took her along a path by the river. After passing a few homes and children too distracted by play to pay them any heed, they came to a large house resting beside the water. Green grass and wild flowers bordered the path, and the red wood of the house's door seemed to soak in the warmth of the air.

As that same warmth seeped into her, Eibhlin sensed something else filling her. Here, she could find comfort, it told her. Before the feeling overcame her, however, she recalled her father crying her name, chilling any kind of warmth in her. She could still sense the desire to listen to the place, though, to let her concerns go. And because she could sense it, she felt discomfort, like placing chilled fingers beneath warm water, a stinging warmth that also causes pain.

Inside, Chensil directed Eibhlin to a room off the entry hall where a beautiful elf woman placed plates around a table. From another room came a younger she-elf carrying a slender flask. Noticing her guest, the lady quickly beckoned Eibhlin to a seat. "Why didn't you announce your arrival, dear husband?" she said, a playful laugh behind her chiding. "I'm too unkempt to receive such a guest. I would've changed had I known."

"I sent Elkir," said Chensil.

His wife almost smiled. "Yes, but when? As you reached the river? You mustn't think five minutes enough difference to prepare both the table and the host."

After a kiss to her forehead, Chensil replied, "Nonsense, Yashul. Both are lovely, as always."

As they spoke, Elkir entered carrying a plate of sliced bread, which the other young elf helped put on the table. Yashul offered Eibhlin a drink as the others sat. The drink smelled crisp as fresh snow and tasted sweet. They passed around the bread and a bowl of fruit as Chensil made introductions. "Eibhlin, this is my wife, Yashul, and our daughter, Elshiran. You have already met Elkir. Yashul, Shira, this is Eibhlin, a human who just arrived through Mealla's road."

"Really?" said Yashul. "If I may inquire, Miss Eibhlin, how did this come about?"

"I'm looking for Mealla, and a fairy I met told me I needed to come here first," said Eibhlin. "But why do you call it 'Mealla's road'? The fairy that sent me here said it was just a normal fairy road."

"It is, and it isn't, in a way," said Chensil. "It is an ordinary door and road and functions as such, but it's also a road Mealla herself made. I don't know that many fairies remember that. They often forget who made which door, but they can feel it, which is probably why there are so few fairy doors in the area. But we remember, and we have kept watch over the door and kept it in good condition precisely because Mealla made it millennia ago. Anything she leaves in the Mortal Realm mustn't be treated lightly."

"Why do you wish to meet this fairy?" asked Yashul.

"I need to speak with her."

"And for that you, a human, entered a fairy road?"

Fairy Door   43

said Yashul. "This conversation must hold great importance to you. But you said coming here was your first step. Do you know your next?"

Eibhlin nodded. "Yes, I think so, but I don't know how to go about it. Chensil, sir, you said you were the 'caretaker' for the wardrobe, right? Have you heard anything about a key?"

"Key?" he said.

"Yes. A special fairy key. The fairy I met said I need to find a fairy key Mealla made. Have you heard anything about it in your work?" said Eibhlin.

"No, I haven't. I'm sorry. If there is such a key in the area, though, I should guess it is somewhere near the door. Fairies usually prefer keeping their treasures within reach, so she wouldn't want it far from the wardrobe, as that is one of the few fairy doors here. I cannot say anything with certainty, though."

"I see. Thank you," said Eibhlin. "I'll just have to look around, then."

For the first time since Eibhlin's arrival, Elshiran spoke. "Shall Elkir and I help you look, Miss Eibhlin?"

"No, I'm fine," replied Eibhlin. "I don't want to trouble you. I can do it myself."

"I advise against that, Miss Eibhlin," said Chensil. "Can you speak any language besides your own? No? Well, there're many here who are the same, many who don't speak your human tongue, many who don't need to. Shira and Elkir know the language, and they know the settlement and people. You, on the other hand, are far from home, child of man. Act with that in mind."

Eibhlin wanted to object, but she couldn't think of a response. "Okay. Thank you," she said.

"Then you can begin tomorrow," said Yashul. "For now, though, you must rest, Miss Eibhlin."

"Oh, no, We can start right aw—!" Eibhlin fell against her chair as her legs gave out beneath her when she tried to stand. Exhaustion raced through her body as if in her blood, her mind suddenly groggy.

Yashul came to support her, saying, "You see? You *must* rest. Direct contact with the Fae's magic is too much for a mortal body and often overwhelms those closely bound to Time. But don't worry. Sleep shall cure you. Come. I shall take you to your room."

Arm-in-arm, Eibhlin and the elf woman went down a nearby hall to a door opening to a clean room with the late afternoon sunlight turning the wood warm to sight and touch. Half asleep already, Eibhlin made her way to a bed covered in thick blankets, flopped down on top of them, and fell asleep. When she woke, she felt more rested than any time she could remember, and all tension in her body was gone. She went to the window. The sky still held tints of dawn's colors, and ghosts of grass stood within a field of mist.

Eibhlin touched the window glass, and then she

noticed her hands. Filthy, covered in dirt, grime, and grass stains, her sleeve, too. Turning to a mirror on the wall, she saw her whole body, from tangled hair to dress hem, messy from the forest and her own sweat, and shame flushed her cheeks. Back home, this much dirt didn't matter so much, not among farmers and shepherds and craftsmen who rarely had the chance to wash regularly, but here, amongst the elves, to dirty such a place somehow felt disgraceful. She didn't want to face her hosts again in such a shameful state, but as the thought crossed her mind, she heard a soft knock on the door.

"Miss Eibhlin," came Elshiran's voice, "have you awoken?"

Eibhlin wanted to pretend she hadn't heard, but that lie, too, made her uneasy. In a quiet voice, she said, "Yes, I'm awake."

"May I enter?" asked the elf.

"Yes," said Eibhlin.

"Thank you," said Elshiran, opening the door. Over one of her arms draped a thick towel, and in the other sat a basket. She said, "Would you care to wash? The bath is ready, should you wish to use it."

The pink in Eibhlin's cheeks deepened. "Ah... yes. That would be nice. Thanks."

With a bright smile, Elshiran said, "Then follow me, please."

"Um, Miss Elf," said Eibhlin, "I... I didn't realize I was so dirty. I even ate at your table and slept in your bed like this. I didn't...."

Elshiran laughed, though it was not a one of criticism, but a happy laugh that shocked Eibhlin too much for her to feel insulted. The elf said, "Thank you for your concern, Miss Eibhlin, but please don't worry over such a thing. If we felt troubled by soil and sweat, we would have cleaned you first, but that would have been out of order. First, you needed rest and comfort. Now you are ready to be clean."

"Yes. Okay," said Eibhlin, feeling again uneasy with the warmth surrounding her. "One more question. Why are you helping me? I mean, why're you so willing to help me?"

"That's a strange question," said Elshiran, genuine confusion creasing her brows. "I'm not quite sure how to answer it. I suppose... I suppose the best way to say it is that it is in our nature, though by that I do not imply that it is against our will. We wish to help you, however it is proper to help, because it brings us pleasure, and because it brings us pleasure, we wish to help more. I haven't yet taken my pilgrimage through the mortal nations, but Mother says there are some among humanity that are the same, who find happiness in giving and helping. Elves are the same, just in greater number." She smiled shyly. "In fact, to feel useless is almost physically painful to us, and to continually act against our nature can lead to unpleasant results. I suppose that's the best I can explain it. Now, I have a towel, soap, and a washrag with me. Do you need anything else? A clean dress, perhaps. I'm sure we can find something that fits you."

"Oh, no, that's fine. I have my own clothes."

Elshiran nodded, and after Eibhlin grabbed her satchel, she followed the elf to a room at the heart of the house where the center of the floor curved down into a deep bowl filled with water. Multiple pillars held up the ceiling, in the middle of which was a skylight sealed off by glass, allowing daylight to sparkle upon the water and reflect white ribbons around the room.

"This is your bath?" said Eibhlin.

"Yes. Let us know if the water temperature is too hot, and we'll adjust it."

"It's heated?"

"Yes. Is there something not to your preference?" asked the elf.

"No, that's not it," said Eibhlin. "But I didn't expect your bath to be, well, like this. It's even heated."

"Of course it's heated," said the elf, confusion again clear on her face. She motioned to the skylight. "Why wouldn't it be? We are very careful to keep our heating glass properly tuned."

"I see," said Eibhlin, trying to sound as if she understood. "I'll try not to take too long."

"Take as long as you need," said the elf as she handed over the basket and towel. Giving a slight curtsy, she said, "When you're done, please place your laundry in the basket so Mother can wash it."

"No, please don't worry about my clothes," said Eibhlin. "I can wash them myself!"

"But did you not want to search for Mealla's key? Would you rather be further delayed by laundry?" asked Elshiran.

"Well, no," Eibhlin admitted. "I do want to find the key as soon as I can, but...."

The elf laughed again. "Miss Eibhlin, you worry too much. You're our guest. Please allow us to serve you."

In the presence of such good-natured laughter, Eibhlin felt her hesitation shrink. "Okay. Thank you, Elshiran. And you don't have to call me 'miss.' I'm not a lady, and we're around the same age, right? At least, comparatively."

With an even brighter smile, the elf said, "Thank you. I'm happy, Eibhlin. Then you shall call me Shira. My full name is a bit long."

Eibhlin felt a smile now tugging at her own lips. "Okay, Shira."

"Now, please, enjoy yourself and relax. I'll go begin preparing your breakfast," said Shira as she slipped through the door.

Taking that warm bath felt like waking up again, dirt slipping away to be replaced by rejuvenation. Once she was finished and had dried as well as she could manage, Eibhlin quickly dressed. She threw on a plain dress and over it a blue kirtle decorated around the neck with beads and embroidered at the hem with birds. It was last year's birthday gift from the women back home and the only thing she owned that felt nice enough to wear around the elves. Walking out to the main room, she saw Yashul seated on a chair and reading to Elkir. She couldn't understand the story, as they spoke in the elven tongue, but the rhythm with which Yashul crafted her voice drew Eibhlin till she was peering over the mother's shoulder at the book.

"Do you have a question, Miss Eibhlin?"

Eibhlin backed away, saying, "No, it's nothing. I was just wondering what you're reading."

"It's a very old story," Yashul replied, "one detailing the life of the elf craftsman, Chimelim. In the ancient days, he fashioned three tools and endowed them with great power: deep, ancient enchantments beyond any remembered today, except perhaps in the Fae. With these tools, he crafted many magical items, each with its own abilities. For his skills, he gained great respect, but he lost all peace as peoples from every nation sought him, whether to purchase one of his works or to learn his secrets. Long he lived, as is the elven nature, but never did he concede to one request, nor take on a single student. He had realized the power of his craft and regretted what he had made. He would not pass such power to another."

"Did he destroy them? His works, I mean."

The lady shook her head. "How could he? What he had made were as children to him. To break them would have crushed his spirit. Instead, he scattered them across both Fae and Mortal Realms, never speaking of them again even as he left this world."

"It sounds sad," said Eibhlin.

Yashul's fingers drifted over the book's script. "Yes. His name, Chimelim, means 'to become filled with much knowledge and understanding,' but at the end of his life, he desired the name Munmelim, 'one who destroys much knowledge and understanding'. His ambition led to much suffering, but perhaps it might yet bring some good."

Eibhlin didn't understand what the lady meant by those last words, but before she could make herself ask for more, Yashul turned to Elkir and spoke to him. He climbed down and ran toward one of the halls.

"Aren't you going to read more?" asked Eibhlin.

"No, not at the moment. There is work to do," said Yashul. "And he only asked to read till you were ready. He's quite excited to search for your key."

"Are you sure you want to let your children help

me? It could be dangerous," said Eibhlin.

"In what way?" said Yashul. "Is it the danger of falling down stairs? Being swept away by a river? Encountering a wild beast? Human child, there is no more danger in this task than in the movements of daily life."

"Maybe I might kidnap them," said Eibhlin.

The lady laughed. "The both of them at once? And for what purpose? No, I should think that too difficult, and even if you should grab one, you would not make it far here in any direction, not without help. Tell me; is your thinking common among humans? It has been so long I cannot remember."

Blushing, Eibhlin said, "You can't be too careful."

"Are you certain?" said the lady. "If, in being careful, you should miss a chance to do good or fail to act when action must be taken, then you have been much too careful. Should you have been too careful, you would not have made it here."

"But if I'd been more careful, I wouldn't even need to be here," cried Eibhlin.

"Child," said Yashul, softly, "do not mistake carefulness for prudence... nor regret for wisdom."

Just then, Shira entered from the dining room. "Mother, I'm sorry to interrupt, but I need your assistance. Everything is just so stubborn today."

"Oh, dear, are they now?" said Yashul, standing.

"Do you need any help?" asked Eibhlin. "I'm pretty good at cooking, or I can at least help prepare ingredients, to repay you for all the help you're giving me."

Yashul guided Eibhlin to a seat. "Miss Eibhlin, do not worry over such a small thing. Repay us? There's no need, though I assure you your kindness is appreciated. Besides, I'm not sure how the tools might respond to a stranger such as yourself. So, please, relax. We shall have your breakfast ready shortly. Now, Elshiran, which ones are causing you trouble?"

"Well, everything, but the worst is the paring knife. It still won't let me use it."

Yashul sighed. "I know the old thing is stubborn, but honestly! What am I to do with it?"

Eibhlin had assumed, based on their interactions, that Elkir couldn't understand her language. However, this assumption soon proved an illusion, for upon touching the correct topic, Eibhlin found his language skills far above adequate.

"And then," exclaimed the child, "Chimelim appeared with his magic claymore forged from a dragon's tooth, the Chaos Cutter, E'imun, and cut the monster in half! Swish!"

"Amazing. So Chimelim was also a strong warrior?" said Eibhlin.

"One of the greatest!" replied Elkir. "Of any that

battled in the Elder Wars, Father says almost no one has as many songs and tales of heroism. He was the greatest elf to ever live."

"I thought Mother and Father said that titled belongs to Melya, the Wise," said Shira.

"But all he did was talk," said Elkir.

"'Wisdom is greater than might.' Didn't Chimelim himself say this?"

"But it's just talking!"

The siblings continued their debate as the three approached the other homes. As before, Eibhlin's eyes looked from one roof to the next. The way they stood made her think of mushrooms or wildflower popping up in clumps. From a wooden tower she hadn't noticed before came a long whistle, followed by flocks of birds darting out from the covered top and breaking apart to go every which-way.

"Maybe the messengers have some information that could help us find the key," said Shira, half to herself as her eyes followed the birds zipping over the grassland.

Elkir jumped forward. "I could ask. I'm fast."

Shira nodded. "Okay. If no one knows anything, ask them to send out a sparrow to ask around the settlement. It can't hurt. Eibhlin and I shall start on the Hall. Meet us there."

Throwing a clumsy salute, Elkir rushed off. Shira

brought Eibhlin back to the building where, just the day before, the human had emerged from the wardrobe. "Father suggested we start here, since this is also where the fairy door is kept," said Shira.

What had once brought wonder now turned to despair as Eibhlin stared at the immensity of the Hall. "How can we ever search it all?" she said.

"By starting now."

By the afternoon, Eibhlin couldn't be more frustrated. Following hours of fruitless searching, they went to check with the messenger station, but all they received was further disappointment and a few curious stares at Eibhlin. Now they sat with their feet in the river on the forest side of the Hall, resting feet tired from walking the seemingly endless maze of hallways, and munching on scones packed that morning by Yashul.

Eibhlin took another bite, allowing the sweet and slightly sour taste to turn her thoughts away from the morning's failure. To one side of her, Elkir noisily splashed his feet as he stuffed his remaining scone in his mouth, while Shira sat on Eibhlin's other side, silently picking away at her scone and placing each small bite carefully on her tongue. Water sprayed into the air as Elkir dropped his feet into the water and let out a long, loud sigh.

"Why'd the fairy have to hide her key?" he said.

Eibhlin glanced at the boy. "You two don't have to keep helping me," she said.

"But we want to help you," said Shira. "We haven't even searched one fifth of the Hall, and do you mean to say you will search the rest of it and, if the key is not here, the rest of the settlement alone?"

"But you should go home and help you mother," said Eibhlin. "She shouldn't have to do everything at home while you're helping me. It's not fair to her. Besides, what if we don't find anything?"

"If we don't find anything before evening, then we will go home, help Mother, and then come back tomorrow," said Shira. "You sound as if all must be accomplished in a single day. Hurrying at the wrong time brings nothing but ill tempers and impatience. Please don't worry so much. It may take days, or perhaps longer, but we'll find your key."

"Thank you," said Eibhlin, feeling a little better.

They had just settled into a comfortable mealtime silence when Elkir suddenly stiffened. "What was that? I think I heard something."

For a moment, the three sat in silence. Eibhlin could only hear birds, the river, and echoes from the inhabited side of the Hall. However, Shira soon stood, saying, "It's from upriver, from the forest! A voice, I think, and one in need of help. Come!"

Before Eibhlin could object, both elves rushed barefoot into the woods, and she, uncomfortable with solitude in that moment, ran after them.

Deep into the woods they ran, and the deeper they went, the more Eibhlin sensed a change. It was not so much in the look as in the air. Eibhlin knew the feeling of enchantment, for her own country held sprinkles of magic, tastes from its fairy visitors, and thinking now, she recognized a similar feeling from the Hall and Shira's home. But the forest beyond the Hall felt different, more ancient. Not so ancient as the fairy road, she thought, though she did not know why, but no less overwhelming for its youth. These woods, these untamed trees, and this pathless undergrowth, held a stronger, wilder power. It felt as if any magic that might be contained and ordered under the skill and wisdom and even age of the elves, now ran free. Eibhlin's forest felt dry as deep winter, while this place was spring in full bloom, full of life and the essence of past ages gathered up and reborn anew. It came in the rustle of leaves, the babble of brook, in the spring of step, the utterance of breath, all things of ancient days forever repeated and revisited as if in their genesis. Fear and wonder and ages and moments so filled her heart with longing, she felt tears gather in her eyes. Even at the forest's most peaceful, the yearning did not lessen but increased. This swirling and pushing and pulling,

Eibhlin could not discern if she should desire it or not. But still she ran, following her guides, trusting in those of surer feet. In that journey through the woods, Eibhlin encountered the essence of the elves, hidden from those who would rather run from than toward that ancient vitality.

The riverbank came in and out of vision, and a sound rose to Eibhlin's ears that she recognized as a voice. Elkir and Shira turned to travel along the bank, eyes searching for the voice's origin. Then, Elkir pointed and shouted, "There!"

A brown shape was floating down the river, and from it came the voice. Shira sprinted to a nearby tree with branches hanging over the water and scaled the trunk with as much ease as if it were stairs. She pushed off the trunk and went along a branch till she stood over the river. Hanging from her legs, she reached down, scooped up the brown shape, and tossed it to her brother.

Eibhlin moved beside Elkir to see what it was when the shape cried, "Oh, thank the Heavens' Maker! I quite thought I would drown this time. Why, if you had not pulled me out, I might have finally cracked, or worse, snagged and broke my strings!"

In Elkir's arms sat a strange instrument of dark, reddish wood and resembling a harp connected to a sounding box. On the instrument's face, silver hummingbirds lowered their heads to a field of aster flowers, flowers that also twisted up the ribs to bloom near the crossbar. A strong, tenor voice rang out from the sounding box. "Thank you for grabbing me from the river. Dreadful things, rivers. Never tell you where you are going and jostle you about as if you should just run along with them. Most dreadful, disagreeable things! In any case, thank you for your help."

Elkir beamed. "Wow! An enchanted kithara. Such amazing fortune. You're very welcome, Kithara."

"It talks," gaped Eibhlin. "The instrument talks."

"Oh, there is a human with you," said the instrument Elkir had called a kithara. "Inexperienced with enchanted tools, Miss? No surprise, really. You speak with the accent of eastern Enbár, and that place is more exposed to Fae magic. Fairies are not usually fond of tools, too much iron involved, if you get my meaning. No, your shock is natural."

Shira, having returned to the group, said, "I, too, am surprised. Why should an enchanted instrument be floating down a river?"

"Great King of the Planets! How could I forget?" cried the kithara. "Miss Elf, is your settlement nearby? I must speak with a person of authority. It's urgent!"

Shira frowned. "Why do you need someone in authority?"

"Dark elves."

Instantly, Shira's face blanched. "We must return. Now!"

Elkir stared at his sister as she grabbed his and Eibhlin's wrists and began pulling them away. As she saw the fear build in the boy's eyes, Eibhlin asked, "What's wrong? What are dark elves?"

Shira shook her head, and her hands trembled. "Not here. We must tell Father. Come. Quickly!"

They dashed back through the wild magic, back to civilization. Upon reaching the settlement, Shira ran to the messenger tower and hurried up the ladders. At the landing, she grabbed the kithara from her brother and ran up some stairs onto the top floor.

Seeing her, one of the messengers came over and began speaking to her. Shira glanced at those around her and then whispered something to him. The elf looked confused, but he went over to a desk and pulled out a small roll of parchment. He asked Shira a question, and her response caused him to drop his pen. She quickly motioned for him to keep quiet, however, and after a tense, whispered exchange, she held up the kithara. Clearly disturbed, the messenger nodded, jotted down the message, copied it several times, and ran off to the bird keep.

Shira returned to Eibhlin and Elkir, saying, "Come with me. We need to wait for the elders at the Hall."

The next hour of waiting passed in near unbearable silence, for none of the group could gather the strength to speak against the air weighted with fear and uncertainty. Finally, Chensil entered the Hall with a few other elves.

"Elshiran, your message held ill news. Are you certain?" he asked.

"Yes, Father," she said. "This kithara spoke of dark elves, and it spoke no lies, though I know nothing more than my message contained."

To Eibhlin, it sounded as if the instrument bowed with its voice as it said, "Allow me, the witness, to speak further, Lord Elf. As you can see, I am but an instrument, one of little use without a minstrel. My minstrel and I were traveling this way with a small merchant train when a band of dark elves ambushed us. I trust I need not detail the horrors that followed. Amidst the chaos, I fell into the river, which soon bore me away. I did not see the battle's end, but I doubt victory lay with us, for those were no mere bandits but a fully armed unit. The Lord of Heavenly Powers bless my poor master. I would mourn him now if not for the current urgency. After the attack, I drifted down the river for two more moons before my rescue. That is all."

Chensil's countenance darkened. He spoke firm words to Shira in elvish before turning to the elders. Eibhlin felt the tension in the air and shivered. After the elders left, Shira said, "Father told us to return and inform Mother. They're going to ready the guard."

Once more joining hands, they all left the Hall in silence.

Chapter 5

The sharp clatter of dishes came from the kitchen. Eibhlin sat in the main sitting room, the kithara lying on the table next to her. As soon as they had returned home, Shira told her mother of the events. Yashul left dinner preparations half-done, charging her children to watch the house while she and their father were gone. Since then, a couple hours had passed, and still no news had come.

Staring at the kitchen, Eibhlin murmured, "Even with the danger, they still leave their children alone."

The kithara spoke, giving Eibhlin a shock. While lost in her own thoughts, she had forgotten about the instrument's enchanted nature. "You need not worry," it said. "There is strong magic within the walls and windows of this house. Only highly skilled sorcerers could break through, and the dark elves are not likely to waste such a scarce resource on a mere civilian's home, not with armed warriors attacking their troops. Do not be so afraid."

"I see. Thank you. I feel a bit better now," said Eibhlin, though her face did not show it. After a moment, she said, "Kithara, what are you?"

"I am an instrument."

"Instruments don't talk."

"No. Most of us do not."

"Then why can you?"

"Ah," said the kithara, "now we reach a useful question. I possess speech because I am an instrument of priceless quality, the eldest instrument still played, crafted a mere thousand years after the Dawn of Time itself. My maker was Chimelim, greatest craftsman among all races and ages, and I am his fourth child. I am Melaioni, Protector of Understanding, Messenger of History."

"Liar," Eibhlin said flatly.

"My good lady," cried the kithara, "you doubt my words?"

Eibhlin replied, "You can't be telling the truth. To find someone... something as amazing as you claim to be, and in the way we did, it's too crazy to believe. It would be too much of a coincidence."

"Coincidence? You think our meeting just coincidence? Good lady, as said before, I am the Messenger of History. I have witnessed kingdoms rise and fall and ages pass from one to the next. If I have learned nothing else, it is that there is no such thing as mere coincidence," said the kithara.

"But—"

"You think it coincidence that my master and I

were waylaid by dark elves that likely now come to attack this town?" continued the kithara. "You think it coincidence that I fell into the river and so traveled here in time to give the elves warning? Do not call such threads coincidence. If you doubt in Divine Providence, call them fate or the work of Lady Fortune, if you must. Only do not call them coincidence. That is but a dream." After Eibhlin gave no reply, the kithara asked, "Have I cleared your mind, good lady?"

"No," she said.

"I see. I am sorry, then, if my words brought only confusion. Have I at least cleared my name? You still think me a liar?"

"I'm not sure," replied Eibhlin. "I think I want to believe you, though."

"If you need sure evidence, the elf daughter can confirm the truth of my claim," it said.

"No. I'll believe you."

"You no longer think me a liar?"

"I don't," said Eibhlin.

A soft sigh, like the lightest thrum of its strings, came from the kithara. "Thank you, my most gracious lady. As the Messenger, to be accused of twisting truth, such a charge near splintered me."

Eibhlin blushed. "I-I didn't—"

"No, no, my good lady. Do not hesitate to speak your mind to me. Honest thoughts matter more to me than kindness, even when painful," said the kithara.

Eibhlin said nothing, but she felt a bit relieved and let her shoulders relax.

Late afternoon shifted to evening, and evening to night. There was no moon. During that time, Elkir had come into the sitting room, shooed from the kitchen by his sister, and sat down next to Eibhlin. He turned through a book, but Eibhlin could tell his mind didn't really process a single word. The kitchen had long gone quiet, but there was no peace in that quiet.

Everything shattered with the crashing of glass. The sound filled the house, swallowing all others. It had come from the bath.

In her fright, Eibhlin couldn't even scream. Beside her, Elkir whimpered. He seemed about to cry when Melaioni hissed, "Quiet!" Just that one word, but with it came terror. Elkir grabbed Eibhlin's kirtle. Eibhlin's own hands locked into fists on her lap. Both stared, unmoving, in the direction of the bath.

So focused and tense was she that Eibhlin barely bit back a cry when Shira appeared and touched her shoulder. Eibhlin almost spoke, but the elf's trembling hand motioned for silence. Shira lifted the kithara from the table and snuck into the hall toward the guest room, beckoning for the others to follow. Slipping off the couch, Eibhlin followed as quickly as she dared, Elkir still gripping her kirtle. The group slid into the guest room. Shira took out a key and locked the door, muttering a few words. A dim glow spread over the door before fading into the wood.

"That should give us some protection," she said.

"What's going on?" asked Eibhlin.

"Dark elves," said the kithara with a voice like a dissonant chord. "I would know this feeling anywhere, sends my strings trembling."

"I thought you said they can't get in here!" said Eibhlin.

"They shouldn't have. I don't know how—" Melaioni broke off.

"What? What is it?" asked Eibhlin.

"It's a new moon!" said the kithara. "Bathing glass naturally has weaker barriers than other windows, due to its purpose, and during a new moon they become even weaker. At the same time, the dark elves are stronger tonight than any other time."

"Why? What's going on?" repeated Eibhlin.

Shira spoke. "They turned from all that is good and are now of darkness. They shun light of all kinds, can stand neither sun nor moon, and they cannot stand their brothers and sisters who would not follow in their corruption."

"And so they want to kill you?" asked Eibhlin, caught between disbelief and horror. Wickedness like that simply didn't make sense to her. It was like something out of her church's Holy Book, like the stories the priest might read on Holy Day from which he drew lessons but which had always seemed so divorced from Eibhlin's everyday life as to be almost fiction. But now those stories felt too close to her to be anything but real. Elkir tightened his grip. Eibhlin had forgotten about him and now regretted speaking.

Still holding the kithara, Shira bent down to take her brother's other hand. "Yes. They wish to kill us. Under a new moon, they have only distant starlight to fear, and now they have entered this house."

"What can we do?" said Eibhlin.

Just then, the door shook, and a snarl slid through the cracks. Curses sounded from beyond the dense wood, and Elkir released Eibhlin to hide in his sister's protective embrace. Once more, and with a stronger force, the door slammed against its hinges. Again and again the door shook, but the barrier held. But the invader beyond had heard its prey. A loud screech pierced the defenders' ears, followed by a sharp snap and more curses. Moments later, the screech came again, but this time the snap took longer to follow. The sound came again.

Screech.

Snap.

Screech. Screech.

Snap.

Screech. Screech. Screech.

Snap.

Screech. Screech. Scree-

Suddenly, the wood cracked in its center, the tip of a blade poking through. Elated cries from the other side chilled Eibhlin's lungs. The door wouldn't hold.

The blade retracted and came again, breaking farther through the wood with a sound like metal striking and scraping against stone. Barely thinking, Eibhlin reached into her satchel and pulled out her knife. She had just unsheathed it when the door split in two, at last sounding like no more than wood. The invader entered the room.

When trying to describe that moment later, Eibhlin would always struggle with the words. The stench of mud and grease, the large eyes glowing as they reflected any small trace of light, the bristling hair on its head and arms littered with dirt, the skin white as the chalk of her own sea cliffs, these she could describe. However, all this paled to the atmosphere spreading out from the creature, infecting the air. All she could say of it was, "Before then, I had never really understood what evil is."

The fallen elf snarled as its clawed hand gripped a sword patterned with blood and rust. Chittering laughter came from its thick throat. Its gaunt chest heaved out raspy breaths between laughs.

Eibhlin couldn't move. She felt distant, as if she were just a spectator. She saw the knife in her hand, heard her own fear-shallowed breaths, but they didn't seem to be hers. She was back home, dreaming before another normal day. Just like always, she would get up, tend to the chickens, make breakfast, go to town in the morning, come home in the afternoon, make dinner, eat, clean, and go to bed. Just like always. Just the same. No monsters, no elves, no quests, no keys, no arguments with her father, no dealing with fairies except for stories and glimpses between trees. It would not be "over". It would never have begun. None of it.

The dark elf tensed like a wolf toward a sheep, an image Eibhlin knew well, and she broke from her daze just as the hunter lunged at her. She stumbled back, and its sword cut her arm rather than her throat. She swallowed a cry. Some years ago, she had been mauled by a wolf, giving her scars on her back, but though there had been more blood at that time, this small wound stung far worse, like being attacked by bees while running through nettles. Pain, shock, and fear almost blacked out her vision, but a collision with a bedside table brought her back to her senses.

The sword struck again, and this time, her body remembered the wolves and moved faster. She dodged to the side and stabbed with her knife, putting all her weight into it. A howl struck her ears, as did Elkir's shuddering whimper. When she turned to the sound, the dark elf pushed her away and ripped the knife from its side. It grunted, threw the blade away as if it were hot, and charged Eibhlin again. She barely dodged the sword and scrambled across the bed, landing on her wounded arm as she tumbled to the floor on the far side. Renewed pain stabbed up her arm to her head and down to her feet. No forced bravado could hold in her cry this time. Eibhlin rolled over, but she couldn't move her legs. Pain paralyzed her. The dreadful laughter filled her hearing again, and she looked up to see the dark elf crouching on the bed over her, sword raised.

Then a firm, clear word echoed in the small room. How it echoed, Eibhlin didn't know. She also didn't know how she could have ever thought she knew speech. That one word felt almost physical, as though it were solid sunlight flittering through the air. She had only been too insubstantial to see it before. All this entered and passed from Eibhlin's mind in less than a second, but even as she processed it, the moment was gone, replaced by a scream so sharp that she flinched.

From the dark elf's chest protruded her knife, and behind the creature was a trembling, tear-faced Shira. The creature tried to face its attacker, but before it got halfway, cracks of light shot across its body like lightening, covering the fallen elf in golden lines with the knife blade at their center. Instantly, the dark elf dropped its sword and began clawing at the marks. It gave one more scream before crumpling over, never to rise. At the creature's death, the dim room appeared to brighten a bit, and the air, though still polluted, grew lighter.

Eibhlin let out her held breath, and had it not been for the pain in her body, she would have relaxed. Her mind, at least, released its tension, and she fainted.

Eibhlin awoke to a mottled green sky. When her thoughts finally caught up to her eyes, she recognized the green as various dried plants hanging from the ceiling. She sat up. It was a small room with two, low windows, one to the east and the other to the west looking out over the familiar meadow and river, letting sunlight pour onto the floor and midway up the wall. Tables sat at either window, and there were a few closed cabinets along one wall and a fountain of water in the center of the room. The water gave the air a cool, sweet fragrance, like the smell of spearmint freshly picked on a midsummer's morning back home.

Home. Though it had only been a few days since leaving, how long those days felt compared to the blurred memories of routine. And yet, they all felt distant in that moment compared to the golden sunlight, the green ceiling, and the clear sound of water embracing her now.

Yashul came through the door. In her arms she carried a set of white sheets topped with a shallow bowl filled with white flowers floating on water. Approaching Eibhlin, she smiled and said, "Good morning, child. Are you well?"

Though questions crowded her mind, Eibhlin couldn't find her voice. Instead, tears gathered and spilled down her cheeks. Leaving the sheets and bowl on one of the tables, Yashul pulled out a handkerchief and began wiping the girl's tears. The cloth smelled faintly of lilies. The lady asked, "Why are you crying, child? Does your wound pain you?"

Eibhlin shook her head.

"Then why?"

All Eibhlin could do was shake her head. She did not know why she cried. Was it fear from the attack? Was it relief? Longing? Sadness? She couldn't decide. It would be many more years before she would come close to understanding that quiet morning in the elves' country.

When her tears finally stopped, Eibhlin said, "I'm all right now. Don't worry. I won't cry anymore."

"Don't be sorry for these tears," said Yashul. "Indeed, I wonder if maybe you did not shed enough, but all shall come in its proper time. Would you like something to eat, child?"

Eibhlin said yes, and Yashul fetched a bowl of broth and some bread. That simple meal, however it was made, tasted better to her than any she had tasted before. A chill she hadn't noticed before left her bones, and a soft peace settled in her spirit. Afterwards, Yashul gave her a cup of water from the fountain, which tasted like the sweet drink from her first meal at that house. Then Eibhlin slept.

A few days passed in this way, with much sleep and little else, but her times awake grew longer every day. During those times, Yashul spoke to her. She heard about how the elven guard confronted the invaders with such ferocity that the dark elves fell into panicked disorder and how, despite the healers' best efforts, a few souls passed beyond the threshold to the Unknown Country. She heard, too, how Yashul and Chensil had returned to find their home torn apart and their children weeping over Eibhlin's unconscious body.

"When I inspected your wound and felt how cold you were," said Yashul, "I feared you too far gone. The dark elf's blade had been made with fragments of moonlight from the Fae Country folded into the metal, and with the Fae in its present state, such material is a fatal poison to children of the Sun, such as men and elves. But Lady Fortune smiled upon you, for the ill enchantments had already been eroded but their use against the door and Shira's spell. There were still several hours till the poison spread beyond treatment. However, as a child unaccustomed to wickedness, the effects on you have lasted longer than most. Don't worry, though. They shall soon pass."

And pass they did.

After the fifth day, most remaining symptoms were gone. That afternoon, Shira and Elkir came to visit. With Eibhlin's recovery near complete, their mother had granted them permission to see the patient. Elkir ran across the room and hugged her while his sister carried over a set of cups, some wafers, and a pot of tea. The drink tasted strange to Eibhlin, like drinking dirt scented with flowers, but she finished what was given to her. The wafers were delicious.

As they ate and drank, they talked about the weather or what so-and-so did yesterday, but eventually the conversation drifted to that night of the attack. Shira's hands shook, and Elkir seemed to lose his appetite. Since that night, their father had been busy. Other homes along the river had also been attacked, some with victims. Council meetings conferred daily, and their father often found himself pulled out of the house as soon as he got back from one project to work on another. It had been several centuries since the dark elves had last evaded their defenses, let alone managed to break into a home.

"I didn't know it was such a big deal," said Eibhlin.

"Father and the elders worry that, in addition to taking advantage of natural weaknesses in our magic, the dark elves might also have a new kind of sorcery that helped them," said Shira. "Any weapons we retrieved, at least, are being examined for new enchantments or variations on old ones."

"I see."

"But," Shira said, "that shouldn't keep us from searching for your key. Elkir and I have been looking and asking around while you recovered, but we haven't found anything yet. Tomorrow, though, you can join us again. I'm sure we shall find it!"

Eibhlin didn't speak. Except for that first morning of recovery, swimming between reality and dreams, she had entirely forgotten about the key. How many days had she spent in bed, asleep? And she had even forgotten the very reason she had come to this place. Gripping her sheets, Eibhlin stared out a window at the saturated colors of late afternoon. "Yes. Tomorrow, let's look some more."

After that, the conversation returned to simpler, happier things. When the two elves left, though, Eibhlin knew her smile was the first false one she had given them. She hoped they hadn't read through that lie. A familiar guilt rose in her chest and colored her cheeks, but she pushed it away and lay back in bed, staring at the ceiling.

Tomorrow. She must find the key tomorrow.

She was awoken before tomorrow came by a soft voice calling her name and a gentle touch upon her hand. Strong, sharp shadows hung about the room. The spring water glistened in the moonlight. From outside, insects hummed and chirped. The sun's world was asleep, the moon's awake, and now, in her waking, she had intruded into that world. She was a foreigner in that world, and she was not the only one that night. By her bed stood Yashul. The lady held no light, but her face shone as if reflecting the moon, and in her eyes was sadness. Yashul motioned for silence, and she gave a smile so tinged with sorrow Eibhlin almost wept.

"I have a request for you, dear child. Will you listen?" asked the lady. Eibhlin nodded. Yashul continued, "Thank you. However, there is one more thing I must ask before I proceed to my request. You must do exactly as I tell you, every part of it. If you cannot make this promise, then I shall leave you now, and this shall all be as a dream."

Eibhlin tensed. "Why?" she asked, but the lady only shook her head.

"I may only tell you if you give me your word. I'm sorry," said Yashul.

"Then I give you my solemn oath to do all you tell me to," said Eibhlin.

The sadness in the elf's eyes deepened so that Eibhlin nearly took back her word, but she held her tongue. "Very well," said the lady. "First, promise to hold secret what I say and do from all who draw breath."

"I promise," said Eibhlin.

"Then," said the lady, "with your word binding you, I may show you this." From the wide sleeve of her gown, the lady pulled out a plain string of twine from which hung a key. It seemed made of crystal. Its surface was smooth, but beneath that surface were countless facets, causing the moonlight to dance rainbows within the body. The hole in the handle was lined with silver, and a soft light came from the key.

Eibhlin's jaw tightened, and her breath caught. The elf nodded. "It is as you guess, child. This is the key for which you seek."

"You had it the whole time?" said Eibhlin. "Why didn't you say anything?"

"It is what I promised, to first judge whether the one seeking the key can be trusted with it. Elves, as those between the Mortal and Fae, can see what might be missed by both. Such was the reason I was asked to fulfill this role, and such was my oath when I took the key under my protection," answered Yashul.

"And you trust me enough?"

"You fought to protect my children. I can think of no better test than the one you have already faced," Yashul replied.

"Then you're giving me the key?" asked Eibhlin.

Yashul took Eibhlin's hands in her own. She said, "Dear child, with all my soul, I wish I could gift you this key. You have already protected what is most precious to me. I could ask no better price. However, proving your quality and obtaining the key, these are two different tasks. The one who gave me this key, the one you seek for reasons that are your own, I gave her my most binding oath. I must not hand over the key without a price. This condition I cannot break."

Eibhlin looked into the elf lady's eyes. "Is the request you have for me related to that?"

"Yes."

"Ask me," said Eibhlin.

Gently, Yashul reached into a basket sitting on the floor and lifted out Eibhlin's blue kirtle. All traces of blood or dirt were gone and any tears or frays mended. In the moonlight, the beads and white birds glowed as if they were lights reflecting off still water. The lady spoke. "This kirtle is wonderfully made. Such love and skill rest within each stitch, and its beauty cannot be disputed. My child, Lady Eibhlin, my request is this: will you give me this kirtle for the key?"

Eibhlin felt her heart pounding in her chest. Her kirtle? Only that? Except, it wasn't "only." That kirtle had been a gift, made just for her. And it was blue. How much had the women of the border town worked and saved to buy cloth of that color? And the time spent making it. Before now, should she have been asked to give away such a thing, she would have refused without a second thought. Before now.

Eibhlin took a deep breath and gripped her sheets. With her heart heavy but her voice steadier than she felt, Eibhlin said, "There is something I must set right, and for that I need to see Mealla. I can't let myself fail when I've hardly begun. So, yes. I accept your price."

The sorrow did not leave Yashul's eyes as she took up the key again. She said, "Then, Lady Eibhlin, one who I have judged worthy of trust, I bestow upon you this key and release it from my keeping. May it serve you well."

Eibhlin's hand sank a little under the key's weight. She pulled it close, feeling the tingle of fairy magic in her fingertips. This was her first key. Taking her own gold chain, she felt a need to bring it and the key near, as if they recognized their similar origins and called for each other. She removed the key from the twine and brought it toward her chain. The chain passed through the solid key, like light obstructed then joined again. She stared in silent amazement at the crystal key strung on the golden chain.

Only two more left.

Once more, the elf wrapped her fingers over Eibhlin's. "I hope your journey succeeds, dear child. May the Maker of Lady Fortune and Father Time grant you much of both. And know, child, that you have my blessing," said the lady, and she kissed the girl's hands and forehead.

"Thank you. I'll remember," said Eibhlin. Then she asked, "Yashul, I knew I could find the first key around here, but I don't know where to go next. Do you?"

Yashul shook her head. "I do not, and that ignorance is of my own will. It is wise not to be too involved with the workings of the Fae and its lords and ladies. But I will not leave you without some direction, nor did Mealla, for she bound each of her keys to a fairy door leading to another key's location. If you find the door this key opens, you can find the next one. She didn't say anymore on the subject than that, and I did not inquire further. However, knowing the day would come when I gave away my key, I searched for an item that can help you."

And with those words, she reached again into her basket and pulled out a simple, brass compass. It was quite an ordinary thing, with a ring on one side to put it on a chain and no engravings or embellishments to please the eye. It had only one notable feature; in the center of its lid was a keyhole.

"This," said the elf, "I obtained on my own, so I may do with it as I see fit. I give it to you, child, as part of my blessing, as a guide."

Eibhlin took the compass and turned it over in her hand, opened it, and looked it over completely. Save for the keyhole, it really seemed to be an ordinary compass. "How can this guide me?" she asked.

Yashul answered, "The compass is enchanted. It can direct you to any lock or door so long as you have the key. Place the key in the compass's keyhole, turn it, and the compass shall point you on your way."

Cautiously, Eibhlin took the fairy key and slipped it into the keyhole. She turned it and heard a chiming click, and suddenly a golden orb of light burst from the compass. It rose up and shot away like a firefly trailed by a thin ribbon of light. In her surprise, Eibhlin dropped the compass.

"Now, open it," said Yashul.

Picking up the compass again, Eibhlin opened its lid and saw the compass needle glowing and pointing in the direction the light had gone.

"Follow the needle's light, and it shall lead you to its door," said Yashul.

"And that door will lead to the next key?"

The lady nodded. "It shall at least be close to where you might find the key."

"Thank you! I'm in your debt," said Eibhlin.

"The compass is a gift, child. There is no need for repayment," said Yashul. Then her smile faded, and the lady's voice grew grave. "And now, Lady Eibhlin, dear child, since you now have the key, you must be on your way at once."

"What?" said Eibhlin. "Why? Can't I leave in the morning? Shira and Elkir have been working so hard to help me. I have to at least show them that I have the key!"

The lady's sadness showed even clearer. "No, child. You must leave at once. You must never tell another breathing soul, whether mortal or otherwise, from whom you received the key. This is a requirement from me for taking my key."

"But why?" cried Eibhlin.

"Being someone who holds Mealla's trust can be dangerous if it is known by the wrong persons," Yashul replied, and she would say no more.

"Can't I at least say goodbye to Shira and Elkir?" said Eibhlin.

The lady leaned in, tears gathering in her eyes, and took Eibhlin in her arms. "Dear child, you mustn't tarry any longer! Even just one day's delay could make your journey harder than you can bear. I have your belongings here. There's no time for goodbyes, no time for proper farewells. You must be on your way."

Eibhlin hated what was being said to her, but she had promised to do as she was told, and she had faced enough broken promises to want to avoid breaking any herself, so she climbed out of bed. The light of the compass felt much colder now. She dressed, and the two made their way through the house, past the family bedrooms and the destroyed bath and to the door. They were in the main sitting room, heading for the door, when a thrumming voice called out to them.

"Would you be so gracious as to tell me where you might be going so late at night and so heavily burdened?" it said. It was the kithara, Melaioni. It sat on a chair, its brown wood reflecting soft silver and blue.

"Curious, Messenger of History, Collector of Stories?" replied Yashul.

"It is my nature, milady, the purpose for which I was made," said Melaioni.

Yashul smiled softly. "Yes, and for your fulfillment of that purpose, you are the most noble of instruments. However, that is a question whose answer I am forbidden to tell any but the one who must receive it."

"Very well. Then I shall not ask again. But if you will not grant me that boon, perhaps you would grant me another?" said the instrument.

"Ask, and we shall see."

"I wish to go with the girl," said Melaioni.

"With me?" Eibhlin asked. "Why?"

The instrument replied, "Why, to record your story, of course. My master is dead. Though I mourn, he shall never come for me. No... he shall never come. Yet I must not stay here, for it is my purpose to find and bring the histories of the world to all who will listen. I can see by the key around your neck that your story is not confined to the Mortal Realm, and long has it been since I have observed such a song in its making. Let me accompany you, milady, that I might witness myself the outcome of your journey, whether good or ill."

Eibhlin hesitated. "It would be wise," Yashul said to her, "to take Melaioni. It knows the world and its events better even than the elves. It could give you advice and company on your road."

There was no arguing her ignorance of the world, and the thought of company, even in the form of a talking instrument, sounded encouraging, so Eibhlin agreed. She took up the bulky instrument and found it lighter than she had thought, and warmth pulsed through it as though it were a living creature rather than an enchanted tool. She slung the kithara's leather straps onto her shoulders and found the warm presence already comforting.

Yashul said, "And now we must separate. I wish

you fortune and speed. I do not wish you safety, for the path you have chosen holds many dangers, but I pray you may pass through your trials unharmed regardless. And know this: should you find the other keys and wish to return here, use all three keys on any fairy door and turn them each one full circle. They shall open the way to their doors, and you can find your way back to us. Now go, Eibhlin. I have delayed you too long already. Dawn comes swiftly."

Yashul kissed Eibhlin's forehead again, and they parted with tears in their eyes. And so Eibhlin left the comfort and rest of the elves, following the needle's light toward the door to the second key.

Chapter 6

The black sky had turned blue before Eibhlin found the fairy door. She and Melaioni had traveled in silence, following the needle downriver to a tall stone. Hidden behind the grass at its base was a keyhole lined with the same golden light that had jumped out from the compass. Eibhlin took the key from the chain and turned the lock. The keyhole let out its brief burst of light, but the crystal key did not, itself, diminish. After returning the key to the chain, Eibhlin stepped forward. The pull beyond the door felt much stronger on this road, but she felt stronger as well and withstood the force without much difficulty. In what could have been hours or days, she arrived on the other side of the road.

The crash of ocean waves filled the air, and she found herself standing in a cave, the slowly retreating tide lapping at her feet. Weariness came over her, and she picked a spot above the waterline to lie down and fell asleep. When she woke, the sun had reached midafternoon, and the heat pressed against her skin even in the shade of the cave.

"Good afternoon, Milady," said Melaioni, sitting

against the rock wall with her bag.

After returning the greeting and taking a stretch, Eibhlin noticed the light still shining from the compass, the needle still pointing to a light-lined keyhole cut into a section of rock still damp from the receding tide. She frowned.

"Do you worry about the light?" asked the kithara.

"Well, I don't want people staring at me because I have a glowing compass hanging from my neck," said Eibhlin. "But I didn't ask Yashul how to make it stop."

"Oh, why, that is a simple task, Milady. Just take the key and-"

"Wait. Don't tell me. I can figure it out. I'd have to anyway if we hadn't run into each other," she said. But after flipping the compass cover up and down, searching its surface, and general fiddling, she still wasn't sure what to do.

"Milady, if I may—"

"Don't worry. I can—"

"Milady," said Melaioni, "did you not want to complete your quest swiftly?"

Eibhlin looked down at the instrument. With a sigh, she said, "Okay. A hint. Give me a hint, and if I still can't figure it out, then tell me."

"Very well, Milady. Consider this: it may be to a compass, but it is also a lock."

"Also a lock... oh!"

Eibhlin picked up her key, placed it in the compass, and turned it the opposite direction as before. It gave its chiming click, and the needle faded back to plain metal and swiveled back to north. The light around the fairy door's keyhole scattered, and the compass returned to its unassuming appearance. Eibhlin smiled.

Meanwhile, the kithara said, "Now, Milady, I advise you to keep that compass on your chain with that key. It is fairy-woven, correct? There is no safer place in the Realms, Mortal or Fae, for them than upon that chain. Well, then, shall we go, Milady? And as we go, please tell me your story thus far."

"But I swore to Yashul that I would never tell anyone about what happened last night," said Eibhlin.

"Are those the exact words?" said Melaioni. "The words used matter when it comes to contracts and magic and their combination. Think carefully."

Eibhlin recalled the events, the exchange, and her promise, trying to remember every detail she could. Finally, she said, "I promised to never tell 'another breathing soul' what was said and done."

Melaioni replied, "I thought as much. Lady Yashul is a prudent woman. I am sure it is no coincidence that one of my titles is 'The Poet That Has Never Drawn Breath.' Carry on, Milady."

The sun shone bright and hot as Eibhlin and Melaioni traveled along the beach, and Eibhlin scolded herself for sleeping through, rather than using, the cooler morning air. For a couple miles, they met no one, but they heard the murmur of sound above the sea and birds. Eventually they saw people walking and riding along the land above the sand. At last, rounding a bend, they saw in the distance a fleet of white sails surrounding a city. White walls with large gates stood between the ships and the tiered buildings, and dark masses gathered at the gates. The sight gave Eibhlin new strength, and they reached the gate and its hoards as the last rays of light glittered on the ocean.

So many people! There was so much movement and talking and shouting and hustling and bustling and too many things for Eibhlin to take in. It was as if all the merchant trains had visited her town and tried to fit into its square all at once. The city sat on an island and had only one land road in, a road quickly thinning as the tide rose, and the tightening crowds seemed to press the air from her lungs.

"There are so many!" she gasped, and she could barely hear her own voice over the noise. As she pushed through the crowd, she tried to keep in mind Melaioni's advice.

"It is nearly time to close the gates for the night," it had said as they approached the crowd. "There will be many trying to enter or leave Leukosica, to leave this city before that happens. You are merely a passerby, a visitor, not a member of a guild or a merchant train here on business or a noble on a diplomatic visit, nor are you staying here for long, so you do not require any official papers. Just announce yourself to the city's customs agent, giving your status as *para*. He will understand and will probably just jot down a pass and wave you through, but I still suggest you keep your head down to avoid unnecessary questions that could make you miss curfew."

With these words in her mind, she now stumbled through the crowd, people jostling her from every side. Her heart pressed against her ribs as she approached the gates. It looked like a mouth waiting to swallow her. She only began to relax after receiving her pass and leaving the shadow of the gate and its portcullis teeth. On the other side, the crowd dispersed, and her breath returned. She looked around.

She took in the mass of buildings of aged white stone turned grayish blue in the twilight climbing up toward a palace at its center. Roads lit by torches branched out away from the gate, people still filling the spaces between shops and homes in the growing dark. Around it all rose the white walls, and on the western side she could still catch the silhouettes of ship masts peaking over the walls. She tried to guess how many people must fill the homes and roads within the walls, but she couldn't conceive of a number that felt large enough. Finally giving up, she started toward one of the roads when a voice called out behind her and an armored hand came down on her shoulder.

Fear spilled back into her. She spun around and saw a pair of guards. Had she done something wrong? Had she made a mistake with the customs officer? Had they thought her a member of a minstrel guild instead of a lone traveler and wanted to see her papers? Had she seemed suspicious in some way?

When the guards started speaking, her panic rose. She couldn't understand them. Words flew at her, but she couldn't respond. After she said nothing for several moments, one of the guards changed his tone, and they started talking between themselves. The first guard turned back to Eibhlin and began slowly listing off countries as questions. When at last he said "Enbár," Eibhlin nodded. A grin lit up his face, and he tossed a few more sentences to his partner before speaking to Eibhlin again. His accent was heavy and not one she could place, but comprehendible.

"You... you are music? No, how do you say? Bard! You are a traveling bard?"

The kithara warmed against her back, and Eibhlin felt obliged to nod. The guards appeared impressed, and another short exchange broke out between them.

The second guard stepped around her and stared at the instrument on her back. He said, "Show us."

Eibhlin tensed, and the first guard reprimanded his partner before saying to Eibhlin, "Sorry. Enbár's words? Language? They are not... common here. He means... means... please play. Please?"

Eibhlin wanted to run, but if she did, what would the guards do? Would they chase her? Throw her out of the city? She didn't even know how to play an instrument, but what could she do under such expectant eyes? Trembling, she took the kithara from her shoulders, hoping as she held the bulky instrument that she could just pass for a mediocre musician and move on into the torch-lit city. However, as she reached to pluck the strings, she suddenly felt calm, and her thoughts slowed. Her fingers slipped from one string to another, sending a soft ballad floating into the twilight. The notes filled her thoughts and flowed from thought to fingertip and back as she played. Once the last notes disappeared, Eibhlin's thoughts returned to sharp clarity, and despite the delight of the guards, cold panic overshadowed her. Giving a curt farewell, she dashed into the city, the confused exclamations of the guards falling behind her.

After a while, she turned from the now sparse road into an alleyway and collapsed against the wall, hugging the kithara to her chest as she caught her breath.

She said, "What... what just happened? Harp, tell me right now!"

"Milady, please recall that I am not a harp but a noble kithara, and my name and vocation is Melaioni," huffed the instrument. "As for what just happened, you need not fear anything. I guessed by your hesitation and how you held me that you did not know how to play me, so I guided you. Small magic like that is fully within my abilities."

"You controlled me!"

"'To a limited extent, yes. However, should you have wished to, you could have easily denied my guidance, and I cannot extend this magic beyond playing me. You see, I cannot play myself, so my craftsman gave me the ability to bestow skill upon my minstrel for the sake of performing my craft. I swear upon my honor as a true historian that I can do nothing else of this kind and cannot do so absolutely," said Melaioni.

"Really?" said Eibhlin.

"I can give no greater oath than that," it said. "Even should my conscience snap like an old string, I would never break such an oath. If you still do not trust me, I apologize. I did not think you would be so frightened. Most are not, after all, to learn they do not need skill to make money. I promise I shall not guide you again without your asking."

"You really won't?" said Eibhlin. "If you do, I'll

leave you sitting on the side of the road. Got it, Mel?"

"'Mel'? It has been a while since I have worn that nickname. But, yes, Milady, I promise," it said. "I do not want to be thrown away. It would be quite unproductive."

Eibhlin almost smiled. She then glanced out to the nearly empty street. Dull blue lay over everything, broken only by orange orbs of torches lining the road at regular intervals. The cobblestone beneath her was cold and the air comfortable. She slumped forward with a sigh.

"Milady, are you unwell?" asked Mel. "Should we not find an inn? In a port city like this, we should be able to find some place that speaks your language, or I can reveal my nature and act as a translator. But we must be quick. The night darkens."

Eibhlin frowned. "I was just going to sleep here."

"What?" the kithara said. "Milady, for a young woman to sleep in an alleyway, what is more in a port city, is not safe!"

"But I don't have money," she said. "When I left home, I didn't think to grab any."

"You did not ask the elves?"

"Why would I ask them for money?"

"What about Mealla's purse? You could withdraw some coins from there," said Mel.

"No!" Eibhlin said. "I can't do that. If I use it, if I

take any money from her, she might not let me return the purse. I've seen that before from merchants, and I can't risk it."

Mel was silent for a time then said, "Very well. I see your concern. It is likely too dark to safely search out a convent, as well. If you really insist on sleeping outside, then you should go up the hill toward the palace or back nearer to the gates where there are more guards."

Eibhlin tried to nod, but a familiar dizziness stopped her. "Just a moment, Mel. I feel a bit lightheaded and really tired."

"Ah, I see. Yes, the Fae did pull quite strongly upon you while on the fairy road," said Mel.

"But I already slept. Shouldn't this have stopped already?" said Eibhlin.

Mel replied, "The Fae Realm has always been quite mischievous, though in the past few millennia or so it has worsened. Ever since the Moon's Rebellion, but that is a story for another time. Anyway, the Fae loves leading travelers astray, so any time travelers from the Mortal Realm enter a fairy road, the Fae tries to pull them off course. Furthermore, the power of the Fae waxes and wanes with the moon. Ever since the dark elves attacked, the moon has been waxing, so the Fae's magic, its attempts to make you stray, is stronger."

"But nothing happened," said Eibhlin.

"Of course not. Lady Yashul's blessing saw to that. There were other factors, but elven blessings, which are under the Mortal Sun, are quite effective against Fae magic. The pull would have to be much stronger to overcome a blessing. In the future, however, we must be careful. The pull of the Fae shall only grow stronger until it reaches full strength under the full moon. When it does, not even a blessing from the Lady of the Sacred Shadow from the City of Ancients could combat the Fae. Elven magic is only under the sun, after all. It is not the sun itself."

"Then is there any way to keep from getting pulled off course?" asked Eibhlin.

"Just what you are doing. Mealla's keys shall protect you. She is one of the few remaining with such power over the Fae, and she is no servant of the Fae Moon. Her magic can overcome, or at least diminish, the pull. If you find the next key, the combined power of the keys might make up for the blessing's weakness. We must still act quickly, though. The weaker the pull, the more likely the protections are to work. So once you have the strength, let us find you a safer place to sleep, Milady. You need to rest away the power of the Fae for tomorrow," said Mel.

With a nod, Eibhlin forced herself up, and by midnight she lay curled up in her cloak in a dark alleyway, deep in a dreamless sleep.

Morning came early in that city. Before the sky cleared itself of stars, carts rattled down the streets, and shopkeepers and bakers prepped and cleaned for that day's customers. Eibhlin woke to brooms scraping against stone. Her body hurt more than when she had slept in her forest, and her muscles complained as she stretched out their stiffness. Melaioni sat right where she had left it.

"Do you think the next key is somewhere in this city?" she asked the instrument.

"Quite likely," said Mel. "Mealla would want whoever guards the key to be near the door, and we did not see any other settlements on our way here. And if it is not in the city, perhaps someone has clues to give us direction. Now then, the best place for sleep and information is an inn, and for that purpose, I have a request, Milady."

"The light was not hers,
But one placed by hands far larger
Than her own, too alive
For her current form to fully
Comprehend, and yet, it was she
Who was illumined."

Coins clinked against cobblestone, tossed by

passersby. In the middle of them, Eibhlin plucked the kithara's strings, her voice rising in the air above the hum and clack of people on the road. When the last note faded, a few watchers clapped before returning to business. Eibhlin gathered the copper coins.

"Not much, but enough for a room," said Mel when they had distanced themselves from the crowds. "If only my plectrum had not been lost when my poor master, Heaven's Maker receive his spirit, and I were attacked. Clearer notes would attract more attention."

Eibhlin shifted the coins in her palm. "Isn't this kind of theft, though? I can't actually play you, and I don't really know any of these songs."

"Not yet, but it is my skill and knowledge, only brought forth through you," said the kithara. "Of course, I cannot stop you from thinking as you do, but if it brings you any comfort, the more you play me, the more the skills and songs will become your own. Soon, you will not need my help to play the basic melodies. The songs themselves shall take longer to remember, but they, too shall come with time."

Eibhlin continued staring at the coins. With a sigh, the kithara said, "Come, Milady. We should find an inn. You can practice in your room."

After finding an inn with decent prices and owners who could understand her, Eibhlin ate a light dinner and ran out the door again. There was only about an hour of daylight left, and she had a key to find. She wandered the area, asking those she met for rumors, strange stories, or whispers of the Fae. Most ignored her. Many didn't understand her, and those who stopped gave no help. When at last the crescent moon rose above the walls and stars covered the sky, Eibhlin returned. The number of drunks had doubled, but they seemed the good-natured type, satisfied with clashing mugs, robust laughter, and off-key singing. She asked a few questions, but to no helpful end. In the end, she went up to her room, practiced on Mel, and went to sleep. Days went by as such. The most eventful moments were the occasional bar fights, but the innkeeper and his wife turned offenders out into the alleyways before they could do much damage. By the fourth day, Eibhlin began to envy the happy drunks from the nearby tables and let out a sigh.

"Still no luck, miss?" asked the innkeeper's wife as she placed down Eibhlin's drink.

The two women had become acquaintances after the second day when Eibhlin helped subdue an aggressive drunk by slamming Mel against the man's gut. The instrument made no effort to restrain its indignation, much to the astonishment of all present. Many, including the innkeepers, assumed Eibhlin must secretly be a minstrel of high status to own such an instrument, with Eibhlin's denials only giving them further surety of their idea. Following the event, the wife started talking to Eibhlin whenever she could. Whether this was as thanks or due to the misunderstanding of Eibhlin's status, Eibhlin did not much care. After elves and enchanted instruments, casual conversations with an ordinary person felt miraculous.

"I can't find anyone who knows anything," Eibhlin said. "The best I got were rumors of fairy sightings and fairy rings a country away."

"Well, I don' really think a fine, young lady such as yerself should really bother with all this fairy stuff," said the wife. "Mighty troublesome. But I suppose it's the minstrel's lot, isn't it, never ta leave these things alone. Anyway, if ye told us a bit more, let us know what ye're lookin' for, me and my husband could help out a bit more."

"Thank you, but I'm not sure I should. Besides, I wouldn't want you getting caught up in 'troublesome' things," said Eibhlin.

The woman shrugged. "Innkeeper's lot is ta have trouble come through yer door. By the way, how's yer harp-ish friend? Still upset?"

"It's worse than 'upset.' Mel is still sulking and won't stop tripping me up as I play. I do that enough on my own. And it won't even talk to me. It wasn't even damaged, but it's acting like I cracked it down the middle," grumbled Eibhlin.

The innkeeper's wife laughed. "Childish instrument, isn't it? Well now, don' go havin' a fallin' out. These past few days, with you two playin' outside, we've had a lot more guests, lots of them because of yer music. It'd be a shame if ye stopped." Then, dropping her voice low, the woman said, "Ye know, miss, it... it might not be helpful, and it's not about fairies exactly, but I know a story ye might want to look at."

Eibhlin glanced up to the woman, signaling for her to continue.

"Well," said the wife, "ye know that tall bell tower near the western wall? Used ta belong ta some monks. Well, I've heard stories that some sort o' creature lives up there. Jumps around from bell ta bell, playing them when it thinks no ones around. It caused so much mischief to the monks that they practically abandoned the place. I know it's not what ye're lookin' for, and I really don' think it's wise ta mess with something like that on purpose, but maybe the creature, whatever it is, could help ye somehow."

Eibhlin finished her drink in one gulp. "Might as well try," she said.

"You have not asked for anything but directions all afternoon," said Mel. "Did you hear something last night, Milady?"

Eibhlin pushed her way through human traffic to

the roadside so she could take in her surroundings. "Have you decided to stop sulking? And don't talk right now. What if someone else hears you?"

"I do not sulk, and there are enough voices around that one more will not draw too much attention. That is, so long as your speaking to yourself does not make you look too suspicious, Milady. Anyway, I simply wish to know where you are taking me. Other than that, I desire no further conversation," replied the instrument.

"Is that so," said Eibhlin, checking a hand-drawn map and matching landmarks. She continued, "Anyway, I don't exactly know if we'll find anything, but the innkeeper's wife said there is some kind of creature living in the western bell tower. It's not much, but it's the best I've got, so I'm checking it out. You're here because you would complain if I left you and you didn't get to 'witness this part of the story' or however you want to say it."

"I suppose your jab at me is true," said Mel with a thrumming sigh. "In any case, while intentionally seeking out an unknown creature is unadvisable, given the present circumstances, there is no better option. The moon grows each day. If we do not find the key soon, we might have to wait a couple weeks till it wanes enough for safe travel."

Weeks. Eibhlin couldn't wait weeks. Already over

two weeks had passed since she ran away. She had to hurry and set things right so she could get back home.

The monastery bell tower wasn't big, but it was larger than Eibhlin had estimated. It was the gray color of stained white. The tower's dark wood roof reached over the city walls, and eerie silence enclosed the area, a pocket without sound hidden along the borders of a bustling city. Eibhlin shuddered, but she forced herself toward the door. The door was made of the same dark wood as the roof and did not have a lock. Its hinges groaned and protested as Eibhlin threw her weight against it. Inside, light pierced through small windows, sharpening the darkness. It smelled like old wood. Slowly, she stepped forward as floorboards creaked and the sound echoed up the tower. Another shiver ran up her spine.

She couldn't understand it. What made this place so hard to endure? Made it so frightening, as if turning her into a child again? A child. Faint memories drifted into her head. She had felt this way before....

Creaks filled the room as she moved to the stairs, one hand on the wall in the darkness. When she reached the stairs winding up the tower, a knot tightened in her stomach. She hesitated. The instrument's voice brought her back again.

"If I may speak, this bell tower was in frequent use

until recently, correct? Do not fear. The bell keepers would have kept the stairs in good repair."

"I got it. You don't need to tell me," said Eibhlin, her voice harsher than she had intended. She hadn't even considered that point, and now that it had been brought to her mind, her eyes ran up the stairs. Even if the tower wasn't especially tall, the upper stairs were still a dangerous distance from the ground floor, and they were not as wide or sturdy as the elves' stairs had been. Eibhlin moved a little closer to the wall and started to climb.

The knot in her stomach did not go away. Instead, it worsened. The feeling from her childhood, that nameless terror, built. This fear, it was different from when she had faced the dark elf. She couldn't explain how, but she knew it was. The darkness, the silence, the smell, it reminded her of Yashul and her elven home, though that may have been due to the differences. Light and forest to dark and stone, laughter and chirping birds to silence and creaking wood, comfort and welcome to disquiet and fear, water and flowers to dust and stagnation. There seemed nothing similar. And yet, somehow, there was. By all rights, this place should make her feel like that night against the dark elf, but no. Somehow, it was like the good lady and her home.

Coolness of stone seeped into her fingers, and her

eyes watched dust motes float in the beams of light as she kept climbing. The higher she went, the heavier she felt. Finally, she reached the landing. It was a spacious place without decoration. On the other side of the room stood another staircase leading to the rafters, and suspended above the floor were a pair of ropes that ran up to the bells. Up here, sunlight poured in from large windows, and some of Eibhlin's heaviness lifted. All she could smell was the sea breeze. Her eyes wandered along the walls and up to the bells. Nothing.

She called out, "Hello? Creature, or fae, or whatever you are? Are you here?"

No reply.

What if the rumor was wrong, she thought, and she felt her hopes sink. She stood like a lost child till Mel's voice came, "If you are not too opposed to it, Milady, I have a suggestion."

"Why do you keep asking me permission? Go ahead."

"I am simply trying to respect your desire for me to remain silent, Milady," said the kithara. "Anyway, I think we should wait until sunset. There is a strong feeling of magic, maybe even fae magic, in this place, so the rumors are not unfounded. Perhaps the rumored creature is nocturnal. Or one that turns to stone in direct sunlight. We should wait to be sure that this place is empty. Also, if I may, I suggest you draw your knife. One must be especially wary around night fae."

Without a word of protest, Eibhlin dug out her bronze blade. Since using it against the dark elf, she hadn't touched it. Somehow, it seemed a different thing now, heavier in her hand. Sitting down, she placed the kithara against the wall and put the knife in her lap. They waited.

Afternoon dragged on, hot but with a salt-scented breeze. As the light dimmed, the deep shadows returned, as did Eibhlin's discomfort. This bell tower, it was like her town's church, she realized. Why had she not noticed it before? This was a bell tower belonging to a monastery, after all. This silence and mix of light and shadow, it was like the first time she remembered entering the church sanctuary. She had been a small child, and as a child she had been frightened of the dark corners as they waited for the candle bearers to finish lighting the altar. It had smelled of incense and old wood, and when the sunlight finally shone through the glass windows and brought light to the air, all her terror of that holy darkness vanished, and she knew it had been fitting to be afraid. What kind of creature would want to live here? What did Mel mean by night fae? A church. Night. Stone. Gargoyles? No, gargoyles were protective. They drove away evil. But if it wasn't gargoyles, then what might—

Eibhlin's blood chilled. Not gargoyles, but maybe something similar. What if... what if it was a demon? Her trembling hands moved toward the knife. Memories, sharpened by the growing darkness, drifted through her thoughts. The small room. The moonless night. Looming shadows. Shira and Elkir, hugging on the floor. The chilling screech outside the door. The first, sickening crack of the door. The dark elf's bright eyes and slithering in-take of breath and unleashed laughter at the sight of cornered children. The blade like a rusty shadow. The poisoned pain. How easily her own blade had gone in. The creature's final, terrible scream. Death.

Outside the window, the last bands of twilight burned across the horizon as the ocean swallowed the final rays of sunlight. Stars heralded the moon. Some other bell tower tolled the hour. Then silence again. A stretch of quiet like a length of twine pulled taut.

"Milady, if I ma—"

Eibhlin screamed and fumbled for the knife, fear and adrenalin deciding her actions. Forgetting to unsheathe it, she swung the knife, thwacking Mel against the crossbar.

"Ouch!" cried the instrument. "First slamming me against someone's stone of a stomach, now striking me with a knife? What have I done to warrant such discourtesy?"

Collecting herself, Eibhlin gasped, "I... I thought you were a demon."

"A demon!" cried Mel. "A noble kithara such as myself, recorder of legends since the First Age after Time's Dawn, a demon? I never thought the day would come, but an insult worse than 'liar' has been thrust upon me! Lady Eibhlin, I insist you rescind the accusation and formally request an apology!"

"I didn't accuse you of being a demon!" said Eibhlin, her face flushed. "I had been worrying about if the thing in this tower might be a demon."

"Teeheeheeheehee! Silly, silly Sunstrands! Thinks demons live with such pretty bells! Teeheehee!"

Eibhlin stiffened at the new voice. Slowly turning, she scanned the room. Nothing. Without quite knowing why she did, perhaps a slight movement barely noticed by her eyes, she locked onto one of the bell ropes and followed it up. Around halfway up she saw... something.

The creature seemed to be a shadow and almost as unformed as smoke. A clear shape could not be made of it. It was small, and two glowing sparks Eibhlin figured were its eyes shined above a thin, white crescent, like a small moon, that was probably its mouth.

Gripping her knife, Eibhlin asked, "You, are you a demon?"

The creature's crescent turned to a half moon, and

it shook so much from its laughter that Eibhlin wondered how it didn't fall from the bell rope. The creature said, "Silly Sunstrands! Silly Sunstrands thinks Vi is demon? Silly! Silly! Too silly! If Vi was demon, Baldtops could have sent him away. But Vi is not demon, so Vi lives with pretty bells."

After Vi had laughed a bit longer, Mel's tenor voice thrummed out, "Are you the only resident of this tower?"

"Baldtops visit. Ring bells. But Baldtops haven't come recently. Vi waits, but they never come. Sunstrands comes, and so Vi waits for her to ring bells, but she doesn't ring bells, so Vi comes down to tell Sunstrands to ring pretty bells," said the shadowy creature.

Eibhlin said, "You mean you waited all afternoon, even when I called for you to come out?"

"Vi was waiting for bells."

"Well why didn't you just ring them?" she demanded.

"Can't. Too heavy," came the answer.

Pointing out the window, Eibhlin asked, "Well, what about those other bells that rang?"

The creature's voice sharpened. "No! No good! Those bells are no good! Not as pretty. These bells are pretty, made with better hands, better hearts. Sound is better. Vi hears it. Vi knows. These bells are better!"

Although she felt the urge to keep arguing, a quick sound from Mel refocused her thoughts. She said, "Um... Vi? That's your name, right? Well, Vi, I didn't come here to ring the bells but to ask you a question. Have you seen or heard anything about a fairy key around here? And not a normal one but one made by a fairy named Mealla. I really need it, so if you know anything then-"

"Sunstrands ring pretty bells now?"

"N-no. I already said I—"

"Ring bells."

"But I—"

"Ring bells."

"I—"

"Bells."

Eibhlin looked over at the kithara leaning against the wall, but it didn't say anything. She said to Vi, "I'm only one person, so I can only ring one of them. Is that good enough?"

"Ring bell," replied the creature.

With a sigh, Eibhlin slid her knife into her bag and grabbed a rope. Bracing herself as she had when she and the town children had rung in the new year that spring, she yanked hard and deep. The rope sank. Then, like a fish on a line, it pulled back, nearly taking Eibhlin's feet from the ground.

Boooong! Boooong!

The sound shook the air. For several rings, Eibhlin let the momentum of the rope dictate her movements. Even when she stopped, the clear, pure sound of the bell echoed in her from forehead to heart, from sole of foot to tips of fingers. In the rafters above, Vi danced about, his laughter rising even above the bell.

"Pretty bell! Pretty, pretty bell!" he exclaimed.

Eibhlin took the chance. "Yes," she said, "the bell is very pretty. Well, Vi, now that I've rung the bell, would you perhaps answer my question? Vi?"

But the strange creature just hurried over a rafter to the bell and hung himself beside it by either hind feet or a tail- Eibhlin couldn't tell which. The creature said, "Pretty bell! Yes, Sunstrands rings pretty bell! Now Vi! Now Vi ring bell!"

"I thought you said you ca—" Eibhlin began, before her voice died in her throat with a gasp.

From some unseen location, Vi, like a street magician, produced a key. The key looked as though of crystal with a bronze-rimmed hole in its bow, and it glowed, covering the side of the bell in a pale, rainbow ripple. Vi pulled back his arm and then swung. The key struck the bell, and the clearest sound Eibhlin had ever heard sang through the air. Clear, sharp, like pure glass, but hard as diamond, unbreakable, immortal. Eibhlin's legs gave out.

As soon as the sound stopped, Vi looked back

down, waving the key in the air. "Pretty bell! Small bell. Vi cannot ring big bell. Too heavy, but Vi can ring small bell. Pretty bell."

Vi struck the bell again, and Eibhlin shivered as the sound passed through her once more. The creature laughed. Eibhlin tried to speak, but her voice would not come out, as if banished by the sound of the key upon the bell. She couldn't move, couldn't speak. Fear resurfaced. What if, on a third ring, she wouldn't even be able to breathe? She did not even have the energy to be startled when Melaioni's voice rose above Vi's exclamations.

"That key, Son of Star's Shadows, my lady seeks that key," it said. "It is our purpose in coming to this tower."

Vi stopped and stared. "Sunstrands did not come to ring bells?"

"N-no." Eibhlin managed, though she sounded a few pitches higher than she had intended. "No. I- we didn't come here to ring the bells. We came looking for any hint to find Mealla's key."

"Mealla?"

"The Lady of Gates and Roads," answered Mel.

At the description, Vi's speck-like eyes enlarged. "Lady of Doors?"

"Yes."

"Sun's Faithful?"

"Among many other titles."

"Lady of Keys who gave Vi this key?" the creature asked, holding out the key in question.

"Yes. That key," Eibhlin said. "Please, Vi, give it to me! I really need it."

Vi swung himself up and scurried back over to and down the bell rope until he was only a few feet from Eibhlin. At that closeness, he seemed even less defined than from a distance. He held up the key. "Sunstrands wants Vi's key?" he asked.

"Yes."

"Vi cannot ring small bell without key."

"Ah. W-well..."

"Vi cannot ring big bell. Too heavy. But with key, Vi can ring small bell. Pretty bell. But if Sunstrands has key, Vi cannot ring small bell, either."

A chill crept into Eibhlin's heart. She remembered climbing the stairs and its fear and the terror of facing the dark elf. This new feeling was somewhere between, though she wasn't sure to which it was closer. She spoke slowly, "Vi, I need that key."

"Even if Vi cannot ring small bell?"

Eibhlin nodded. A moment later, she wished she had not. Vi's eyes grew till the glowing orbs filled most of his smoky form, and his mouth stretched across his face, thin as the first sliver of moonlight after a new moon. Starting from her chest and spreading to the rest of her body, Eibhlin froze, as if her heart were pumping ice.

Vi spoke. "If Sunstrands wants Vi's key, then bring Vi something else. Bring something else to ring small bell. If Sunstrands brings something good, then Vi will trade."

"And if I don't?"

"Then Vi will eat your thieving heart."

Eibhlin's voice withered to a squeak.

Melaioni yelled, "Eibhlin, wait! Don't spea—"

"She has already spoken, Child of the Knowledge Speaker. Now, Sun's Daughter, Vi will wait three days. Bring Vi new ringer of bell, and Vi will trade Vi's key. Come tomorrow or tomorrow's tomorrow or tomorrow's tomorrow's tomorrow and ring bell. Vi will answer and see what you have brought."

With that, the creature dashed back up the rope and was lost amongst the shadows. When the creature did not appear again for several minutes, Eibhlin stumbled to her feet, picked up Mel, and hugged the instrument close as she began down the stairs. Halfway down, it vibrated against her fingers as it said, "Be careful of the steps, Milady. There is very little light."

In almost a whisper, Eibhlin asked, "Are you talking normally to me again?"

"Would you rather I keep silent?"

"No. Thank you." She went down several more

steps before she spoke again, grabbing the first topic that came to her thawing thoughts. "You called Mealla 'Lady of Gates and Roads' and 'Sun's Faithful' and stuff like that. What did you mean?"

"Mealla, or rather the fairy you call Mealla, is one of the eldest in both the Mortal and Fae Realms. Some believe she might even be one of the few remaining who were born at the Dawn of Time, though there is no way to know for sure. As for her titles, powerful immortals tend to get those. If you ever wish to hear the related stories, just ask. I cannot play myself, but I can at least tell the stories," replied Mel.

Eibhlin's voice trembled. "I made a deal with a pretty powerful fairy, didn't I?"

"Yes."

Gripping the instrument tighter, she asked, "And what about Vi? What kind of creature or power is he?"

"I am not sure," came the answer. "The full nature of the Fae and its creatures are still unknown to me. Honestly, Milady, the Fae itself is beyond me. But in this case, it does not really matter how powerful or of what race he is, does it? Either you satisfy him, or you die."

Chapter 7

The next two days did not pass well for Eibhlin. Each day, she rose early to sing and play till her voice hurt and her fingers blistered. Then, with what money she did not need for her room and board, she spent the afternoon rushing between markets, bartering for whatever she could afford to offer Vi in exchange for the key. Copper, glass, wood, stone, shell, she even managed to get a good deal on a silver spoon made by an apprentice silversmith trying to get his work out in the market. But both nights, when she brought her options to the creature, Vi refused most of them without even a test. More than once, he simply tossed the item out a window or swallowed it whole, wasting Eibhlin's hard-earned money.

It was now the third day. The noontime sun glistened off the sweat dripping down her cheeks. There was no sea breeze that day. Only heat and humidity. Almost no one walked the street. Not surprising. Today was the weekly Holy Day. With the mess of recent events, Eibhlin had lost track of her days. Now the streets lay almost bare, nearly every shop was closed, and it was her last day.

"I don't suppose fae take Holy Day off," she muttered.

"Not when they have prearranged business," said Mel. "At least, the ones that gamble with people's hearts do not."

Eibhlin plucked the strings with a plectrum. After yesterday, her fingers had stung so much that when she saw a wood shop on her way to the bell tower that evening, she stopped by and requested the item based on Mel's descriptions. As it was the end of the day, the woodcrafter kindly accepted whatever Eibhlin could pay and made a rough tool from some spare wood. Then, after Vi had rejected everything else, Eibhlin offered him the pick. It, too, was rejected, but unlike everything else that day, he did take it, shimmy up the rope, and tap it against the bell. When it barely made a sound, the creature slid back down and quietly placed the plectrum back into Eibhlin's hand.

"Too small," he said. "Too thin. Can't ring bell. Will break, and then Vi can't ring bell. Tomorrow, bring Vi something better, or Vi will eat your heart."

The creature then climbed out of sight. He had shown that much interest only once before, with the silver spoon. However, even that he rejected for its own faults.

Rubbing the pick between her fingers, Eibhlin said, "I wonder what he wants."

"Pardon, Milady?"

"Vi. I wonder what he wants. A silver spoon and a wooden pick, what do they have in common? They're made of different stuff, and they're used for different jobs. And what do they have in common with the key? What made him consider them as a replacement?"

"Maybe he does not 'want' anything. Maybe he is just tricking you, pretending he will trade the key when really nothing will satisfy him, and he is just having some fun before he eats your heart," offered the kithara.

"Thank you for that encouraging thought, Mel," replied Eibhlin. "But I can't exactly act like he is, can I? Besides, I don't think he's just pretending. At least, whenever he actually tried an item, I couldn't help but believe he's entirely serious."

"Hmmm. Yes. I see your point. In any case, you should take a break, Milady. There do not seem to be any potential customers, and it is lunchtime. It is hard to focus on playing well if you are too hungry or thirsty," said Mel.

Nodding, Eibhlin picked up her satchel and returned to the inn. She slid into her usual seat, and the innkeeper came over with a plate of simple food and drink.

After Eibhlin thanked him, the man said, "My wife's been worried 'bout ye, miss. Said the cloud's been over ye since visitin' that bell tower, worried she's done somethin' wrong ta ye."

Eibhlin rubbed her palm against the tankard. "Thank you," she said, "but she didn't do anything wrong. I'm just facing a bit of a problem. Don't worry too much, though. By tomorrow, or I guess tonight, everything will be over, one way or another."

The man frowned. "Got yerself in some sort o' trouble?"

"More like a riddle. Don't worry. I'll figure it out."

With a bob of his head, the innkeeper said, "Well, I ain't got much of a head for riddles, not my wife, neither, but if ye need help, just ask 'er. 'M sure she'd appreciate it."

"Thank you, but I'm afraid it's something I have to face by myself," said Eibhlin, and the man walked away with a nod.

After that, Eibhlin sat in silence, the universal language of Holy Day.

She glanced at her satchel. Inside lay the magical purse, the door to Mealla's incredible wealth. More than once, Eibhlin had toyed with the idea that maybe, just this one time, she could take something from it. Mealla's key, after all, seemed made of diamond or crystal or something similar. Maybe she could find something like either of those. However, she dared not risk it. Should Mealla refuse to take the purse back due to Eibhlin's action, the entire journey would be worthless. What was more, considering Vi's actions, the material or rarity of the item didn't seem important, at least not very. Silver was precious, but wood was cheap. Material, shape, monetary value, none of those seemed the deciding factor.

Reaching into her bag, Eibhlin took out the spoon and the plectrum. Her food remained pushed to the side as she studied the items. Think. There had to be something. Some connection. Eibhlin took up the plectrum again, turning it over, rubbing its surface, searching its grain as if it held the answer.

"Bring Vi something better," the bell tower's inhabitant had said.

"Better." What was "better"? Vi had used that word before, when they had spoken that first night. What did he mean by "better"?

As she turned the wood over in her fingers, she turned the word over in her mind. Suddenly, she dropped the wood, and it clacked upon the table just as she jumped up from her seat.

"What is wrong?" asked Mel.

Eibhlin didn't answer but remained staring at the items sitting on the table. Could it be... it seemed a bit far-fetched, but it was also the only connection. But if it was as she guessed, her situation was hopeless! There was no way she could find a place that sold something with those qualities open for business, not on Holy Day. And even if there was, there was no way she could afford it. She couldn't- wait! There was! There was one thing!

Shoveling the trinkets back into her bag, Eibhlin said, "Master Innkeeper, I need to go. If I come back, I'll play whatever you want. If I don't, don't bother waiting for me."

The innkeeper could only give a confused nod as Eibhlin gulped down her drink, shouldered her bag and the kithara, grabbed the bread from her plate, and took a bite as she raced out the door. Before they had turned the first corner, Mel asked, "What quickens your steps, Milady? Where are we going?"

"The bell tower! I think I figured it out. I know what Vi wants," said Eibhlin.

"Really, Milady? And you say to the tower. Then you already possess the worthy item?"

"I hope so," Eibhlin said. She looked up at the early afternoon sky. "I hope so, because I don't think I'll get any more chances."

When they reached the tower, the sun had already reached the halfway point of its descent. After catching her breath, Eibhlin began up the stairs, pushing down the now familiar, though still disquieting, feeling welling up inside her. She reached the top with her chest burning, and her legs gave out, causing her to slump against the wall.

"Milady! Are you well?"

Ignoring the kithara, Eibhlin forced herself back up, shuffled over to the bell rope, and yanked it down before collapsing again. The bell boomed through the room and out into the air.

Vi showed no resemblance to Eibhlin's hurry as he climbed down the rope, headfirst like a lizard. He said, "Sunstrands is early. Early is good. Has Sunstrands found something better?"

"No," said Eibhlin. While the instrument on her back gave several exclamations in dissonant notes, she continued, "At least, not in the way I was thinking before. Instead, I found what you wanted."

Eibhlin reached into her bag, digging to the bottom, and pulled out her knife. Removing it from its sheath, she held it out so that the blade formed a thin wall between her and the fae creature.

"Does Sunstrands wish to battle Vi?" the creature asked. "Is that why Sunstrands holds knife at Vi?"

"No. It's what I'm offering you, the 'better' item."

The smoky shadow, slightly transparent in the sunlight, said, "Knife? Why does Vi need knife? Knife is for killing and cutting. Vi does not need to cut, doesn't need knife to kill. Why should Vi want knife?"

"Because it's exactly what you want," she replied.

"You always know what you want, and when you have it, you stick with it. No one comes to ring the bells here anymore, but you refuse to go live in the other bell tower. Why? Because you don't want just any bells but these bells, the 'better' bells. The question, then, is why do you want these bells? The answer is the same for why you want this knife. This bronze knife was given to me as a present from my father, the first thing he gave me after my mother died. He isn't that good at making blades, but he made it so that I could protect myself if I was ever alone and in danger. My father is a blacksmith of well-known skill. He's no legend, but merchants are always willing to pay a good deal when he has things to sell. What's more, he has a kind heart that loves what he does, and he always acts with the good of others in mind. This knife was made by my father, a skilled and experienced blacksmith, with my protection in mind. Better hands. Better heart. That's what you want, isn't it? Well, here it is."

Vi shifted on the rope. "Better hands. Better heart."

Eibhlin nodded. "This blade is pretty strong, too. It won't break anytime soon."

The creature twitched out a hand-like shadow and snatched the knife away. Vi scrambled up the rope. He struck the bell. It rang. The note was sharp and sweet. It didn't match the sound of the key, wasn't even close, but before the warm sound had vanished, Vi struck again, tittering as he exclaimed, "Pretty! Pretty! Pretty bells!"

Eibhlin called up, "So, Vi, do we have a trade?"

The creature stopped. "One more thing."

The color fled from Eibhlin's face before returning with gusto. To think she had trusted—

Before Eibhlin could respond, Melaioni vibrated against her back. "What is your request, Child of Moon and Stars?"

"Sunstrands rings bell."

The tone, the calmness of the voice, made Eibhlin catch her breath, and sadness gathered, unbidden, in her heart. "That's all?" she asked.

Vi answered, "Sunstrands will leave after Vi gives you key, just like Baldtops. Ring bell. Just one time. Vi wants to hear big bell one more time."

Without a word, Eibhlin took the rope. The sound of the bell rang out across the quiet streets, strong and clear and alone.

When Eibhlin and Mel left the tower, the second key shone upon her chain.

Chapter 8

Eibhlin returned to the inn right before sunset, when the solemnity of Holy Day lifted with festivity. Pubs and taverns flowed with free—or in less pious establishments, cheaper—drink, and laughter echoed in the evening air. The innkeeper's wife beamed as Eibhlin entered, and the girl could barely finish dinner before the master of the house asked her to make good on her promise. Late into the night she sang and played for the packed inn. Epics, tragedies, comedies, bar songs, even a few requested hymns, Eibhlin no longer needed Mel to guide her fingers for some of them, except on more advanced bars, and her own voice rang out and above the others. Morning found several men still sleeping across the tables and chairs and floor. Most had gone home during the night, and those few who remained either had no wife or had forgotten to fear her during the singing and camaraderie forged by drink and song. The master and his wife were slipping between tables, cleaning what they could, when Eibhlin emerged from her room, tired but packed and ready.

The wife looked at Eibhlin's bag. She asked, "Did

ye find what ye were lookin' for?"

"Yes," said Eibhlin, who felt the keys tingling against her skin.

"Then ye're going now?"

"I can't stay."

"Ye won't tell us anything?"

Eibhlin only smiled and shook her head.

"Well, at least come by and play for us every now an' again," said the woman, her husband giving a gruff second.

Eibhlin addressed the innkeeper, "Before I leave, here's the cost for last night. I forgot to pay it before."

The master shook his head. "Last night's music was enough. Best ye get goin'. Gonna be a scorcher today."

Eibhlin stared at the older couple and saw a shine in their eyes that was somehow familiar and, like Vi's voice the day before, filled her with sorrow and longing. "Okay. Thank you," she said. "If I ever make it back here, I'll definitely stop by."

She waved at the two as she walked through the still-waking streets. That last morning in the city felt just like her first, she realized. She had come, played an enchanted instrument, met a fae, nearly lost her life, and now had a second fairy key. A lot had changed. And yet nothing had. The next day, everything returned to how it always had been.

"I'm pretty unimportant, aren't I?" she murmured.

"How so, Milady?"

"Well, it's just, growing up in a town like mine, everyone is important. Something changes for one person, and sometimes it's almost like everything changes. But here? Here, it doesn't matter what sorts of adventures you have. Travelers come; travelers go. Everything goes on as normal," she said.

"Hmm. Yes. Such can be the case with towns and cities. The more people you have around you, the more distant you become and the more insignificant you feel. Though I would hesitate to say the latter is as true as the former. As the saying goes, a single gust can change the aim of a thousand arrows. Do not overestimate your existence, but do not take it for granted, either," said the instrument.

They passed through the gate by midmorning, and Eibhlin wandered a bit away from the city, making sure she was out of sight, before sliding the key into the compass face. She turned it, the lock clicked, and the ribbon of light shot out and away quicker than thought. Eibhlin took a leisurely pace in following.

Surf pounded against sand, and the salty wind played with her hair and clothes without obstructive crowds or invasive scents. The girl removed her shoes and felt the sand melt beneath her feet at the ocean's summons. "Come home," it said. "Come home."

Not yet.

Soon. But not yet.

For now, she chased that golden thread along the border of the world.

The compass led to the cave where she had arrived from the elven country. However, the needle pointed through the black, deeper into the cave.

"Keep the keys out," Mel told her. "They will give some light."

Eibhlin took out the keys, and their glow looked like twin stars inside that cave, creating a small area of light in front of her. She journeyed into the dark. Down, down they went, leaving both day and night behind. Here in the cave, neither sun nor moon existed, only the stars shining upon Eibhlin's chest. Sound vanished except for the scuffle of shoe on stone. The smell of the sea lingered, but the walls felt dry. The ocean would not reach that part of the cave for several more hours, if it did at all. In the meantime, they went down, down, down through the earth.

And the deeper they went, the longer they passed through unchanging darkness, the more unnerved Eibhlin became. The sun. She had never known before how much she loved the sun. Not until knowing that darkness pressing around her. She held the keys tightly, as though they were candles in danger of going out. So long as the keys stayed alight, the darkness could not touch her. They would keep her safe. Safe until the ascent, when she could return to the sun.

But down they still went. Deeper and deeper. Down into darkness and silence.

"I wonder why she put two doors in one cave," Eibhlin whispered.

"Most likely for convenience," the kithara said quietly. "Fairy doors can only connect like things, such as a rock by water with another rock by water. If she has two destinations she can link in the same area, it saves time looking for another match."

"That sounds so troublesome," said Eibhlin.

Eibhlin imagined the instrument shrugging as it said, "Not really. The hardest part is keeping track of what 'like things' means between materials. For instance, with wood, geography does not matter, as it does with stone, but it must be the same kind of tree, such as two beech trees. When problems really start is when inattentive people of any race or nation accidentally use a fairy's door in their crafts. Indeed, there are more fairy doors just sitting in their homes than people realize. It can be a source of either amusement or consternation, depending on the fairy, neither of which tends to lead to good results. Not to mention when the unwitting owner accidentally falls through the door. Trust me, Milady, when I say the crafting of a fairy door is the least troublesome part about it."

The two fell back into silence, and the darkness continued hugging their light, sneaking into Eibhlin's heart, filling the silence with its terrible whispers.

Just then, Eibhlin slipped. She dropped to the cave floor, and Melaioni scraped against the wall and hit the floor with a sickening sound. Eibhlin hurriedly brought the kithara into her line of sight, her voice echoing in the gloom. "Mel! Are you all right?"

Eibhlin cringed when she saw the scratches along the kithara's side, and her stomach sank as she looked down and saw a large crack running up the instrument's sound box. Tears threatened her eyes, and her throat tightened. She wanted to say something, knew she should, but her mind went blank.

"I will be fine, Milady," said the instrument. Its voice sounded like strings being tightened. "I am enchanted. It will patch itself up soon enough. I probably should not be played much, if at all, for a couple weeks, though."

Eibhlin nodded.

Silence stretched between them before Mel said, "You should watch your step more, if you do not mind my mentioning, Milady."

"It's dark," came the mumbled reply.

"You were never this clumsy on the stairs of the bell tower."

"Those were stairs."

More silence.

When the instrument spoke again, its tone sounded amused. "You know, Milady, with how far down we are going, you might just get to meet your demons."

"What?" said Eibhlin.

"At this rate," replied Mel, "we might just make it to the Gates of the Underworld, like the heroes in the old legends. Then you can see all the demons you want, Milady."

"Who said I want to meet demons?"

"But at the bell tower, you seemed quite eager to assume anyone was a demon."

"That doesn't mean I want to meet one," replied Eibhlin.

"You do not?" said Mel with mock disbelief. "Just as well, really. Nasty creatures, demons, but can be dangerously charming. How did you mistake Vi for a demon, Milady? Demons are not even of the Fae. The fae people were formed of the quintessence while beings such as demons and angels are pure spirit. They are not even of the same nature. Did you not learn that in your histories?"

"I know. I... I was just... I couldn't think straight," said the girl.

"Were you scared?"

"What?" Eibhlin paused a bit before saying, "Yes. I... I was scared."

"And are you scared now?"

Eibhlin tensed. "Why are you asking?"

The instrument's voice, while still strained, softened. "Eibhlin," it said, "I am an enchanted item. I experience emotions such as happiness, anger, and, yes, even fear. However, they cannot impede me as do yours. If you cannot think straight, let me straighten you. Speak with me, Eibhlin. Let me help you. I am just a tool, an item. I cannot help you unless you let me."

There in the dark, deep in the earth without sound, without sun or moon or stars, without any companion but a talking instrument, Eibhlin felt something crack. It was like at the elven home, being healed and treated, when Eibhlin first woke up and wished she was home and remembered her fear. Was it the solitude? Was it the dark? Was it the knowledge that, in that place, the world only existed within that little sphere of light?

What did it matter?

"Don't be sorry for your tears. Indeed, I wonder if maybe you did not shed enough." The elf lady's words came back to her, and Eibhlin could only let the tears fall. Her quiet sobs echoed in the dark, sounding so distant and sad to her own ears that she couldn't stop.

Time did not exist in that orb of light on the border of the Underworld. Eibhlin cried, and Time did not exist to tell her for how long.

When Eibhlin's weeping slowed, Mel asked, "Are you afraid, Milady?"

"Yes," Eibhlin said. "Yes. I'm afraid."

"Do you want me to help you?"

Eibhlin looked over at the instrument. Through her own broken voice, she said, "Yes. Yes, I do. Help me. Please, help me, Mel. I'm afraid. I'm afraid, and I don't know what to do."

With the softest tones its damaged voice could muster, the kithara said, "Well, Milady, first you need to stand."

Eibhlin did.

"And now step forward. Carefully now!"

Eibhlin took a step.

"And now another. And another. And another. Good. Now another step. Good."

And so the pair continued their descent into the heart of the earth.

After the nothingness of utter darkness, even the smallest hint of light becomes more precious than all the gold in the world. When she saw it, the keyhole looked to Eibhlin like the sun. She ran toward the light with a joyous cry. It sat in the wall of stone right about the level of a normal keyhole. Around it, the stone was strangely smooth, and when Eibhlin touched it, she felt the keys against her chest shiver. At once she wanted to fit the key into the lock, but Melaioni's voice stopped her. "Before traveling through the fairy door, you should eat something, Milady. The moon has grown stronger now, and if your body and mind are weak, then you will be pulled aside and lose your way."

Eibhlin felt hunger gnawing in her stomach. During the trip down, she had drunk water, but the anxiety and fear had kept her from eating much. Now, with the exit hopefully in sight, her relief brought with it hunger.

After the quick meal, Eibhlin took out the key and slid it into the keyhole. The door opened, and she stepped through. This trip was much like the others except the pull had grown exponentially stronger, much more than Eibhlin expected, and she nearly stumbled off her way. It was only the two keys and Yashul's blessing that tethered her to her path. She realized this as she came out on the other side of the door. But she had other, more immediate worries to consider, so the thought did not stay long.

The other side of the door did not come out in a cave but on a mountainside staring out toward more mountains, with a narrow, wooded valley below. It was a good-sized ledge, so there was little chance of falling, but it was colder even than the underground, and the air was thinner than Eibhlin had ever known it could be. There was no moisture in the air, either, so it was sharp to her throat and lungs, but refreshing to taste compared to the heavy air of the cave. However, the sudden change shocked her, and she started coughing. After a few minutes, she began adjusting, and her breath evened a bit, but she didn't move. While her lungs were adjusting quickly, her eyes were not, as they had suffered a much harder shock: cloudless daylight after so long in near total darkness. If Eibhlin hadn't had the light of the keys and the compass in that darkness, she might have been much worse off. As it was, her eyes and head ached, so she sat down on the ledge till her eyes could get used to Time's Marker again.

This took several minutes, or it would have if the magic of the Fae had not grabbed hold of her and sent her to sleep. Stars and moonlight shone such cold light upon the mountain that Eibhlin could almost feel it as she shivered awake. Immediately, she dug out her cloak. As she did, she was shocked to see her breath in the silver light.

"Isn't it summer?" she stammered. "Have I been gone a whole season?"

Mel, with its voice noticeably less strained than

when she had entered the door, said, "No, Milady. Summer it still is, or you would have frozen to death up here. I tried warning you not to sleep before you collapsed, but the Fae had pulled too strongly. Look. The moon is over half-full."

"What!" the girl cried, staring up at the snowy half-circle. "Wasn't it only a quarter when we left the city?"

"Yes, but who knows how long we were underground? Certainly not us. What is more, the Fae managed to pull us off course. Oh, it could not turn us from our destination. You need only look at the compass's light and the keyhole beside you to know we are where we intended to be. However, being misled can be more than just losing your way. We have taken a long time to get here, Milady, with the moon and its effects growing every day."

Eibhlin's stomach sank. "Then we might get lost next time! If we lose our way, how can we get back?"

"If it is not too far, you could follow the compass, but if we are sidetracked too much, we might have to track miles, or worse, we could get lost in Fae."

"What should we do, Mel?" Eibhlin asked.

"First, we should climb down the mountain a bit and see if we can find some shelter," Mel said. "Up on the mountain, it is cold, and if a wind starts up, then, summer or not, you might freeze as you are now. There is also the chance of wild beasts and maybe even goblins."

"Goblins?"

"Underground monsters. Similar to dark elves only blind and, while less vicious, far more devious."

Eibhlin gripped the keys as she had during the descent into darkness. She did not want to meet goblins, especially since, if she did, she didn't have a knife to protect herself anymore.

"So, you see, Milady," continued the kithara, "either option, staying here or climbing the mountain at night, neither is a safe nor desirable option. However, I advise at least finding a cleft in the rock or something with which to protect against the cold."

Nodding, Eibhlin locked the compass, and the comforting light dissolved. She then pulled her cloak close and made her way to the cliff edge. On one side of the ledge, a thin path climbed down the mountain. With one hand holding the cloak tight and the other pressed against the mountainside, she scooted along the path, not daring to lift her feet.

After a short while, the path turned into stairs. Seeing the obvious craftsmanship, Eibhlin paused. Someone had made a road to the fairy door. Whether this was good or bad, she couldn't know, and she hesitated till a chill wind crashed into her, tearing open her cloak and nearly knocking her from her feet. She crouched down, pulling her cloak closer until the wind had passed. She looked around. During her climb down, she hadn't seen a single nook or cranny, and if all mountain winds were like that one.... Keeping low and close to the wall, Eibhlin slid down the stairs, freezing both inside and out every time a new wind hit her. Finally, she reached the bottom stair and landed on a level shelf that widened as it bent with the mountainside. Still skirting the wall, Eibhlin came around the bend, and what she saw gave her the same emotions as when she arrived at the keyhole shining its golden light in the dark.

A monastery! The house of refuge stood away from the cliff on a wide ledge, its roof and stone appearing gilded with silver in the moonlight. A small garden and a well sat to one side, both covered and protected, and standing before them all, as if a heavenly sentry, stood a tree.

Such a tree none could think to be of the Mortal Realm. Long, drooping branches, like a willow's, swayed in the wind. Tipping the branches were pale green leaves that looked as if covered in velvet or made of feathers. White and silver flowers in the shape of seven-pointed stars adorned the tree, and every time the wind brushed them, it almost seemed to carry away some song too wonderful for human ears and a perfume that Eibhlin felt she had smelled before, long ago, but which she could not name.

Eibhlin drifted to this tree. As she neared it, she felt the sensation of the keys against her chest strengthen, though with a different music than when she neared their doors. She reached out and let the leaves brush against her fingers. They felt like goose down and warm to the touch. Eibhlin took another step forward so that they touched her cheeks.

"Careful!" said Mel. "This tree is a fairy gate!"

Eibhlin jerked back. "What?"

"This is a Tensilkir, a rare tree of the Fae Realm. Its presence here has enchanted the ground and air. Have you not noticed how much gentler is the wind and warmer the atmosphere? These are trees of protection and strong magic. When brought into the Mortal Realm, they also become doors to the Fae. If you are not careful, it will pull you through, and then where will we be but lost in the Fae?"

Eibhlin backed away. "But... but why is something so dangerous here?"

"It's only dangerous when approached without care," said a deep voice from beyond the tree.

Through the floating branches, Eibhlin saw a monk standing in the doorway of the monastery. His umber habit blended into the dark, but the white cord around his waist, his shaved head, and his silver-streaked beard caught the light and almost glowed. He stepped out over to the tree. Taking a tendril tenderly between his fingers, he said, "Though she is dangerous, like the Fae itself, I hope you don't misunderstand this tree. Just as beauty does not always mean safety, so too does danger not always mean evil. This tree protects us and calls to those who are lost, guides them here, where they can find shelter and direction. And I see by your face, child, that she is calling you."

"But I'm not lost," said Eibhlin.

"Is that so?" said the monk with a knowing smile. "Well, then I must warn you, for then this tree's pull shall be all the stronger, for the lost are not the only ones she calls."

"Who else does she call?" asked Eibhlin, feeling the tree's leaves brush against her cheek.

"Those who wish to enter the Fae," said the monk.

Eibhlin's chest tightened. "But... but I *don't* want to go there."

The monk stared at Eibhlin with dark eyes that made her wish the wind would stop breaking the silver wall between her and the old man. She gripped her kirtle, feeling the keys beneath. In one sense... perhaps she did want to enter the Fae Realm. After all, she had to find Mealla, and if that meant going into the Fae, then so be it. Though she had grown up as a witness of fairy mischief, Eibhlin had never feared fairies and their country. But now....

Eibhlin shivered as she remembered Vi.

She said, "No, I don't want to enter the Fae. I don't want to go there, but I have to. Though not here. Not now. Here, now, I would get lost. I must find a different way."

"I see," said the monk. "If that is your road, I mustn't stop you but rather help you on your way. And for that, would you like some rest, dear daughter? I told you, all who come to this tree are guided, whether because they are lost or because the Fae calls to them, and all who come to this monastery are welcome. Come. Eat. Sleep. Tomorrow, we shall see how my sons and I can help you find your way."

"Your sons?"

"Yes. I am Ormulf, abbot of this monastery," replied the monk.

"Oh! I-I didn't realize... um, honorable sir"

The abbot chuckled. "No need for such formality. While you're here, I am your father."

At his words, memories of her own father's anger before she left came into Eibhlin's mind, but she held her discomfort inside. Outwardly, she said, "Okay. Thank you, Father Abbot."

He led her into the monastery, saying, "Please be careful on the steps. I apologize. I didn't have time to light a lamp after I realized you were outside. I worried the tree might tempt you too far if I didn't hurry. If you will just wait here, I shall go fetch a lam-"

"Father Abbot."

Eibhlin couldn't be sure due to the shadows, but she thought that, for a moment, the good father's smile stiffened. However, the impression passed, and he turned to address another monk carrying a small oil lamp so that the newcomer seemed enveloped in a halo, like the painted saints Eibhlin saw in her village church.

"Brother Callum. We have prayers in just a few hours," said the abbot. "You should be sleeping."

The man answered, "Father, the wind kept my mind awake, though my body wished to sleep. In hopes of bringing peace to my thoughts and heart, I rose to pray. Then, I heard voices in the courtyard, and my curiosity overcame me. I apologize."

"No, don't be sorry, my son," replied the father. "If restlessness holds you, then you can help us. This child shall stay the night. Would you go prepare a light meal and ensure the guest room is ready?"

"Yes, Father Abbot."

The monk's sandals padded against the stone floor, echoing as he left. The abbot addressed Eibhlin again, "Brother Callum, a good man and no stranger to the order. He was an orphan found and raised by my predecessor and joined the order at an early age. I do fear he is a bit on the overzealous side."

"He seemed fine," said Eibhlin.

The abbot only smiled.

The meal was indeed light, just a cup of goat milk and a bit of bread and cheese, but the nearby fire warmed Eibhlin's bones, and she hadn't had milk since she had left home. She nibbled her bread as she watched the flames crackle in the hearth. In the back of her mind, she heard the abbot call her but hadn't understood what he said. She asked for his question again.

"I asked for what reason you've come here, my child. By your speech, I know you are of the southern countries, and yet you have come to this place. Perhaps you would tell me why?" said the abbot.

Eibhlin shifted in her seat. Somehow, the way he called her "child" felt so different from Yashul. What was more, the desire to speak the truth bubbled up in Eibhlin, but something twisting in her chest prompted her to choose her words carefully, though she didn't know why. "I... I am a traveler. As you say, I'm not from here. My home is in Enbár."

"So far?" Abbot Ormulf said. "What business could a daughter of the green hills have in the Northlands?"

The conflict in her soul returned. She felt urged toward truth, but the strange feeling halved her honesty. "I have relatives up here. My mother came from one of the merged towns, the mining towns where humans and dwarves work together."

Again, the priest appeared shocked. "One of the merged towns? Near or away from the sea? Near? My child, you have wandered far from your course if you traveled to here from Enbár attempting to reach one of those towns."

"It wasn't a direct trip," Eibhlin said. "I had some other business to take care of, which I did before coming here. I'm just passing through, and really, I need to be on my way tomorrow. As you said, I've still got some distance to go."

"You are traveling so much by yourself? That is dangerous work, dear daughter, and forgive my impudence, but you have barely entered womanhood," said the abbot.

Eibhlin watched the licking flames and the occasional pop of dancing sparks. "I know. But I must."

"And what business would drive you to such a dangerous journey? You mentioned a need to enter the Fae?" he asked.

Again, Eibhlin felt pressure to tell the truth clash with some sense of caution. "I... I'd rather not say. But please, believe me, Father; when I say I'm only passing through, I mean it. Tomorrow, I'll be peacefully on my way."

Eibhlin and the father faced each other. The girl saw the firelight reflect in the monk's eyes, veiling his reactions and thoughts. At last the priest broke away and stood, saying, "Of course I believe you, my child. Now, the night deepens, and you must be in want of sleep. I shall show you to the guest room."

The room in question was a quiet chamber furnished with a single bed and one small window letting in the moonlight. Once left alone, Eibhlin put Melaioni on the stone floor and flopped face-down on the bed.

"Well, that was a good performance, Milady. I had not thought you so capable at it, and I cannot say I much approve, but that was skilled lying," said Mel.

Eibhlin kept her face to the mattress. Lying was easy. She knew it, had known it for years, and hated it. However, this time.... Turning toward the instrument, she said, "When I was being questioned, I kept feeling like I really wanted to answer, but another feeling kept holding me back. It was... weird. Almost like having two voices in my heard pushing against each other, trying to crush the other."

The kithara took some time to respond. "We should leave here as soon as we can, Milady. It is too dark and cold now, but as soon as daylight breaks, we should be off. I am not surprised by your account, Milady. I do not like how this place feels. It is not right."

Eibhlin frowned. "What do you mean? To me it feels just like anywhere else."

"Exactly."

"Mel, that doesn't—"

"Pardon me, Milady, but monasteries are supposed to feel different. Monasteries, churches, ruins, all sorts of places like those, they have a different- what is a good word- a different 'atmosphere,' I suppose. Surely you realized this yourself, after the bell tower."

"What has the bell tower to do with this?" Eibhlin asked, her fingers gripping the sheets.

"You see, Milady," the instrument answered, "places, be it due to their age, events connected to them, or their uses all possess an unseen element to them, call it a 'spirit' or 'atmosphere' to the place, for lack of a better word. It cannot be seen, but it can be felt. Most humans can feel it when young, but many either allow their ability to perceive this spiritual reality atrophy as they grow older or fail to train the ability in the first place. I, however, have not. This monastery does not have the atmosphere of a monastery."

"So there's something wrong with this place?"

"Indeed, Milady. Something very wrong."

Eibhlin turned over in silence. Dark elf attacks, a heart eating creature, darkness and cold and wind, and now a suspicious monastery, when would these trials end? She hadn't even gotten to say goodbye to Shira and Elkir.

A pang of guilt hit her. Twice. Twice she hadn't said goodbye. When she felt the guilt turning to tears, Eibhlin pushed away her thoughts and memories. This wasn't a time to cry. She had to sleep. But try as she might, she could not summon that elusive thing. Thoughts and memories and Mel's uneasiness swirled together in a storm of confusion and emotion. Even outside it sounded for a moment like the wind broke through the tree's barrier, chilling her room, and she tossed and turned in the night. A couple hours later, the door to her room creaked open. Eibhlin stiffened. The soft pad of bare feet on stone approached her, but before she could decide what to do, Mel's tenor struck her ears and made her tumble off the bed in fright.

"WHO ARE YOU, AND WHAT BUSINESS HAVE YOU WITH MY LADY?"

The intruder yelped, and Eibhlin heard a sharp clang and another cry of distress as whoever it was scrambled to gather whatever had been dropped. There was nothing for Eibhlin to use as a weapon in the room, and her satchel was on the other side of the bed, but she crept around the foot of the bed. She made out bare feet and a habit that looked black in the lack of light, and as she came around the last corner, there was a monk cleaning what looked like liquid off the floor with his habit. Beside him, Eibhlin could just make out a dented lamp.

Taking a breath, Eibhlin stood and hissed, "Who are you? What do you think you're doing, sneaking into my room? If you don't answer immediately, I'll call

Father Ormulf and—"

"No! No, miss, you mustn't call him! Kick me or beat me or curse me, but for your own sake, don't yell or call for anyone!"

"Who are you?" Eibhlin demanded, though she kept her voice quiet.

"It's Brother Callum, miss," came the answer. "We passed each other earlier, but with the abbot present, I couldn't speak with you."

"So you snuck into a young woman's room? Not exactly proper for a monk."

"Who's that?" the monk whispered, looking around the room.

Eibhlin said, "That's my kithara, Mel. It's enchanted."

Callum moved toward the instrument and stared. "You mean this strange harp speaks?"

"Kithara, sir monk, but yes, I do speak," said Mel. "I am an instrument of immeasurable quality, the eldest existing instrument, crafted a mere thousand years after the Dawn of Time. My maker was Chimelim, greatest craftsman among all races, all nations, and all ages, and I am his fourth child. I am Melaioni, Carrier and Protector of Understanding, Messenger of History."

The monk's tone turned respectful. "Ah! A work of Chimelim! I apologize; I didn't recognize you. Oh dear!

Now you really must leave immediately. If he realized you're enchanted, good instrument, he'll sell you for sure to some horrible master."

"'He'? 'He' who?" said Eibhlin, her nerves tensing again and the twisting in her chest returning.

"The Father Abbot!" said the monk. "No, please, you must give me a chance to explain, but we must do that as we leave. Already, I'm afraid we may have been too loud or that the abbot might not be as deeply asleep as I hoped. Please, come! I'll explain on the way."

When the three were down the hall a bit, Eibhlin whispered, "Okay, what's going on? If you don't tell us, I'm going back to bed."

"Oh, please, miss, don't. You mustn't! I will explain all I can, but first I must know, did you come to this place through Ásdagr's door? The door of the Lady of Gates?" asked the monk.

Eibhlin's breath sharpened. "Do you mean Mealla? And how do you know about the door?"

While glancing around a corner, Brother Callum replied, "Is 'Mealla' what she is called in your country? Well, Miss Eibhlin, all the monks of our monastery know about the door up the mountain, for we were granted this place for our monastery in exchange for promising to protect the door and Ásdagr's key."

"The key?"

The monk slipped around the corner, and Eibhlin followed.

"So, you do want the key, though I suspected as much when I saw you come to this place from the direction of the stairs, rather than the mountain roads. There's nothing up there but the door, and the one with a the key to that door most likely wants the next one." Callum said. "Unfortunately, you won't find the key here, but I will speak of that soon. Anyway, our order was meant to protect the key and to give it to one we think trustworthy, should such a figure appear. The records of those who have received the key from us are a secret known only by the abbot, and it seems that every time one of these persons died, the key, through some other magic, always returned. But it has been at least a few centuries since the last time this happened, and in that time, the monastery forgot its duty. The stairs leading to the door were worn away by the wind and frosts, and the monks here became indifferent to their task regarding the key. The previous abbot, Abbot Allan, attempted to restore the order to its proper state and even rebuilt some of the stairs, but, to the detriment of all, he passed before any lasting changes could be made. Worst of all, however, was the establishment of Brother Ormulf as Father Abbot, for not only did he abandon the reforms of Abbot Allan, but he then sold the key!"

Eibhlin felt sick. The key! It should have been here. She should have been so close. "Who did he sell it to?"

Callum stopped, and even in the scarce light Eibhlin could tell he wore a shame-filled face. His voice cracked, "To a fairy your country calls Arianrhod."

"What!" Eibhlin and Callum flinched as the kithara's shout echoed down the hall.

"Mel! Shush!" Eibhlin hissed.

The instrument quieted, but its strings tightened and creaked in anger. "He sold Mealla's key to the Witch of Hours?"

"Yes," said Callum. "He did."

"Witch of Hours?" Eibhlin asked.

"Arianrhod is a wicked, despicable witch! A fairy who betrayed her own people and helped the Fae Moon rebel against her Sun thousands of years ago. Now, the Fae is sick, and instead of repenting, she has worsened her sins countless fold by practicing black magic of all kinds. There is no fairy more wicked than she, nor any living being who hates Mealla more, for Mealla has opposed her since the rebellion," said Mel.

"And now this witch has the key?" asked Eibhlin.

Callum nodded.

"But why? Why would she want it? She's not searching for the others, is she?" said Eibhlin.

"Most likely just because it is Mealla's," said the kithara. "The Witch of Hours hates Mealla, and hatred does not need a good reason to cause trouble for its object. What I want to know is what the Abbot received for it. Brother Callum?"

The monk looked over to the nearest window, which let in a pale glow. He answered, "The tree. The Witch gave him the tree."

"The tree? The Tensilkir? The one that calls those wishing to enter the Fae?" said Eibhlin.

"It does call those," said the monk, "but mostly it calls the lost, both mortal and fae. They then find their way here and, through various forms of trickery and traps, Ormulf evaluates them, and if he approves of them, he sells them as slaves to the goblin mines."

Eibhlin's breath caught, and Mel swore without apology. The girl tried to piece together her thoughts. "He sells... goblin... what kinds of tests? What kind of person is he looking for?"

"Those who will not be missed for a while, I expect," said Mel. "Milady, did he not seem interested in your status as a solitary traveler? And remember you said that during your conversation you felt pulled in two directions? The abbot may have used some herb in the food or drink or some enchantment to make you speak more freely than you would otherwise."

Callum slowly opened a door to a dark hall and glanced inside. Apparently satisfied, he pulled out his oil lamp and lit it, motioning for Eibhlin to follow.

His voice became a strained whisper, "What does it matter how he does it or why? No matter what foul tricks he employs, he only condemns himself further. He has fully abandoned the duty he swore to keep when he became Father Abbot, sold his responsibility to a defiler of both Realms, and with his actions afterwards, he has exchanged the road of angels for the path of demons! He deserves to suffer for eternity within the eighth circle, tortured and made sport of by the very demons he heeded!" Brother Callum then gave a sad sigh. "We of the order can't even stop him. The tree prevents us from leaving. Only the abbot and those who have come after its planting can come and go as they please. We are protected from dangers from without, natural and monstrous, but what good are we if we cannot protect others from the danger from within?"

By now, Callum spoke in choked sobs. Eibhlin stood behind the man, a tangle of fear and sadness. "You're helping me," she said.

Callum shook his head. "One of the few, the very few. Abbot Ormulf thinks none resist him any longer. In fact, for a few years, no one even knew his secret, so were we, too, deceived by the snake. When we began to learn of his evil, those who confronted him directly were either given to the goblins or turned to his side. The rest of us did as I do now, warn travelers when they arrive here and try to send them away. Most laugh at us, and some have even reported us. After a few more of our order disappeared, many of the remaining became too frightened to keep fighting. I am now one of the few who still watches during the night and moves within the shadows. That's why I saw you approach, Seeker of the Key."

"The key! That's right, the key. Brother Callum, thank you for helping me escape, but please, do you know how I can find the Witch of Hours?" Eibhlin said.

"I had feared you might ask me that," said the monk. "Please, miss, I beg you, don't go to that dreadful lady. I wish you safety, and if you should go there, if I send you there, how shall my conscience rest?"

"Then you know the way?" asked Eibhlin.

With a sigh, the monk said, "Come."

He led them through the halls, warning Eibhlin to watch her step. There were traps, he told them. Not deadly in themselves, but ones that would alert the abbot to their movement. The group crept down the halls, and by the time they reached the front door, Eibhlin had begun to notice things: a line of light on the floor where it should be dark, an odd stone here or there, and other subtle signs of the monastery's ill purpose. The group at last made it outside. Under the bright half-moon and the glowing tree, the stars and the tepid air, the whole ordeal seemed a dream.

"Come, this way," said the monk. He led her to the tree. "You must enter the Fae through here."

"Through this tree? Does it lead to the witch? Are you sure?" asked Eibhlin.

"How can I be?" replied the monk. "I've never entered myself, and my brothers who did never returned. However, every new moon, the abbot travels through here, and if he isn't seeking the witch, I don't know why he would enter the Fae. Even if it leads to somewhere else, you must enter the Fae, for that is where the witch lives, and this is the only doorway I know."

"He is right, Milady, and if we are to act, we must do so now. I do not think that if that abbot plans to sell you he will wait till tomorrow night. Most likely, he has already called his 'business partners' and only awaits their arrival. We must go while he is still unawares," said Mel.

"Such is the truth," said Callum. "I fear time is short. If you wish to leave, whether by the road or through this door, you mustn't delay."

Eibhlin looked up at the half-moon, and unease crept along her skin. She could already feel the door pulling her, could feel the Fae. She wished she could wait, but wait she could not. Stepping forward, she said, "I'll take the fairy gate."

Nodding, the monk said, "Very well. Then take this." He pulled from his habit a small penknife. "It isn't much, but it's iron, and iron protects against and hurts the Fae better than any other metal."

Eibhlin took the knife. "Thank you."

"Now be off! Before your chance is wasted!"

"Stay safe, Brother Callum," said Melaioni.

"Yes, please stay safe," Eibhlin said.

Callum smiled. "As I'mim wills, and may His protection rest upon you and guide your steps. Farewell, Miss Eibhlin."

With a sign of blessing, he sent them off, and Eibhlin ran straight through the doorway.

Chapter 9

Eibhlin wasn't even awake when she passed through to the other side of the door. She remembered running forward, brushing against the weeping branches and star-shaped flowers for longer than she thought possible, but when she started wondering why she had not yet reached the trunk, something struck her mind, jagged auras blurring her vision. Her stomach lurched, and she fainted. When she woke, all she could see was black. Soon, however, her eyes adjusted to the hints of light around her, and she saw black branches in such a tangle they could never be untied.

She shivered.

Sitting up, she heard and felt the drip of water and realized she had been lying in a shallow pool. Vegetation and mud clung to her hair and clothes. From behind her came a dull gargling sound. She jumped. Then she brushed against leather straps, and with a cry she pulled Melaioni from where it had fallen face-first into the water. It was half-covered in mud, and water dripped down the sound box. After wiping down the instrument as best she could, Eibhlin brought out her keys. Soft light spread around her.

They were in a swamp. Black trees stood everywhere, their branches either drooping to sweep against the water or reaching up to cover the sky. Moss hung from branches like ragged hair. Water covered most of the ground, turning the land into an archipelago. There were no natural sounds, so every movement Eibhlin made seemed to break some unspoken law. Her nerves tightened. No sound. Hardly any light. But there was a smell and a taste to the air: wet, earthy, old. Yes, old. That was the word she sensed. Old and hard and cold and forbidden.

This was not a place for mortal men to come.

Eibhlin shivered again. "Where is this place?" she asked.

"Fae country."

Eibhlin yelped at the sudden reply. She might have run off if her legs had not given out. With a splash, she collapsed into the water. Trembling, she glared at the kithara.

"I do not believe I have done anything to deserve such a look, Milady," said the instrument.

"You scared me."

"A leaf would have frightened you just then," said Mel. "And rightly so. Never trust a leaf in the Fae country unless you know its tree. But enough of that for now. I suggest we see if we cannot get a fire going. Probably not, since the ground is likely too wet for dry branches, and breaking a live limb off any tree in the Fae is usually fatal. But may as well try."

There were no dry branches. Even if there had been, Eibhlin's tinderbox was soaked. Instead, she had to settle for wrapping herself up in her cloak, the oiled surface of which had repelled most of the water and kept it partially dry.

Eibhlin looked around again. "So this... this is the Fae Realm?" she asked. "Not at all what I had expected."

"Most of the Fae does not look like this," said Mel. "This... well, I suppose we should be grateful. Brother Callum appears to have a good intuition; this is Arianrhod's realm. Most likely, that tree we travelled through is a door leading right to the Witch's house, but we must have gotten pulled off course. Instead of landing on her doorstep, we are lost in her swamp."

Pulling her cloak closer, Eibhlin said, "It's really dark."

"Dark? Oh, the dark is hardly the swamp's fault. It is this dark because it is day. Now, now, no interruptions, please, Milady. Yes, it is day. Ever since the Moon rebelled, night has reigned in the Fae, and for her aid to the Moon, the Witch was given her name in your tongue, Arianrhod, the 'Silver Wheel.' This swamp, too, is the Witch's doing. Black magic. Even if she were not known for it, the trees speak of it. See how black and brittle their bark is? Sick. Diseased. Poisoned by the black arts. See that one over there that looks to have ink dripping from its branches? That is a Tensilkir, the very kind through which we just traveled, only the one at the monastery is healthy, overflowing with health, even, while that one... Milady, it has been centuries since I have seen trees this corrupt."

Another shiver traveled Eibhlin's spine as Mel went silent. She grasped the keys in her hands and pulled them to her forehead, holding their light close. She shut her eyes so that all she could see behind her eyelids was their glow. With her vision sealed, she couldn't see the cage of trees trying to suffocate her. But she could still feel them. Something in the air chilled her lungs, sent fear pulsing through her heart.

"Mel," she whispered, "I'm scared."

"As am I, Milady."

"Can you play me a song?"

"Milady, I believe I have mentioned before that, as skilled and noble an enchanted tool I may be, I cannot play myself. Try as I might, I cannot make even passable music without a player. No. I cannot play myself. Furthermore... Milady, I... I can tell stories, but... but, oh shame, I cannot hold a note."

"You're a tone-deaf instrument?" Eibhlin said, almost with a laugh.

"Milady, please, it is simply the state of things. Whether by accident or a joke or to keep me humble, it is how my maker made me. Rarely has it caused trouble, so I have learned to accept it, but now... now I cannot do as you request, which is far more painful than the crack and scrapes from the cave. However, if you want, I could tell you what to play. Perhaps it will not bring as much comfort as listening to someone else, but I promise it shall give some. Oh, and please be gentle, Milady. The time lost on the fairy road sped the process along, but I am not yet fully healed," said Mel.

With a nod, Eibhlin took up the instrument and began to play. Much as with her first attempts—how long ago those now seemed!—the kithara guided her fingers. Notes drifted through the breezeless air, and for a moment, she let those solitary sounds drown her. Just as Mel said, it did not do much to comfort her. Even though the crack in Mel's body had shrunk considerably, the notes sounded strange, and she dared not play anything complicated for fear of further damage. But even that little bit of comfort gave her a little more courage. Not much, but enough.

After a while, weariness came over her, and she closed her eyes. In her dreams, the song continued. Sweet and distant, like good memories. Eibhlin sat on someone's lap. She rocked back and forth, and a voice sang along with the music. The voice was terrible: off key, breaking constantly, and almost comical in its effect. But Eibhlin loved the voice. She lay back and listened. Soon another, deeper, richer voice joined in. Still she rocked, finding safety in the arms enfolding her. A hand touched her head, stroking it gently. The girl looked up. Two faces smiled down at her, a man and a woman.

The man she knew. How could she ever mistake those sparkling eyes and that dark, bushy beard? He turned to the woman and kissed her hair, whispering something Eibhlin couldn't hear, but she understood that expression, had seen it many times before. It was strange, though, lacking the sadness she always saw within that soft smile. Even so, she knew this man.

The woman on the other hand... for just a moment she thought the woman was Yashul, for the kindness in her smile was the same, but the woman was different. She was human, with eyes like the ocean and hair the color of early morning sunbeams.

Tears pricked Eibhlin's eyes. She knew this woman. She knew she should be sad, should miss her, and sometimes she did, but most of the time she simply couldn't remember this woman enough to feel those emotions. Here in dreams, however, memory took hold and dead loves rose again.

What was this woman's name? What... what....

The dream faded before the answer came.

Her waking was no less dreamlike than her sleeping. Eibhlin opened her eyes to see beams of violet-tinged silver cutting through darkness and multi-armed figures standing as black pillars around her. She sat up. The sharp play between shadow and light chilled her, for the light was cold and the shadows endless. Wherever they stood, a void appeared, and not so much as a breeze came through to disturb the reflections in the black and silver water.

When she couldn't bear the sameness of the swamp, she looked up, and she gasped. Staring down at her was the smooth face of a giant, full moon. It looked unnatural. No dark shapes along the surface, just bright silver with a violet tinge to its glow, and the darkness beyond. There were no stars.

"Mel," she said, fighting back a cry. Her heart pulsed in her chest, the keys shivering against her skin.

"I am here, Milady."

"The moon. It's full."

The instrument made a sound of agreement. "Yes, she is, but then, she always is in the Fae. Ever since her rebellion. The Moon is full every night and proclaims herself ruler of the visible heavens, and every dawn the Sun struggles to climb above the horizon."

"I don't understand."

"I cannot do justice to such an epic without reciting it in full," said Mel, "but in short, the Moon became jealous of the Sun. She did not want to remain his queen, so she gathered an army and rebelled. The Sun, for all his wisdom, loved the Moon too much and fell. Since then, the Moon has ruled the Fae, and the world became ill beneath her wicked, false light, for though she claims to rule the Heavens, she still only reflects the Sun. She was meant to complete him, complete the heavens, but she wanted more, a wish that by her very nature she cannot fulfill. The Fae has always been dangerous to the foolish, but it used to provide clarity to the wise and healing to the humble. Now, it drowns in chaos. It is a place unfit even for its own people."

"Then what about me?" asked Eibhlin. "How do I... how can I...."

"Do not despair, Milady," said Mel. "One thing you must never do is despair. This darkness is deadly, but there are ways to fight it. Your keys are one, formed by one whose power predates the rebellion, and the light they give repels the Moon's shadows. The elven blessing, too, shall help, as it is under a Sun in his proper place. There is little the Fae Moon can do against you directly, but I still advise caution.

"After millennia of her rebellious light, those used

to or born under the Mortal Sun find the Fae Moon's light and the air she touches poisonous. Even with your protections, this effect can only be slowed. If we tarry too long, the poison shall spread and overtake you. Furthermore, do not think the Moon your only danger. The Fae was dangerous before, and as the Witch of Hours shows, it has only grown more so since. But we have waited too long already. Lo, the Moon continues her vain march across the sky. I suggest we not rest while she does so. Her servants bathe in her light and so move in awareness as if it were day. You should not sleep while they wake."

Eibhlin nodded and pulled her things together. As she took a few items from her pack to eat, she remembered Callum's gift. Finding the iron penknife, she tore the hem of her dress and tied the knife to her arm. That knife was her only protection. It was too dangerous to keep it in her bag.

When she finished eating her soggy bread, she asked, "Should we try and mark this place, Mel?"

"Do not bother," replied the kithara. "There is no door here, and even if there was, the woods likely would not let us find our way back. No, best find Arianrhod first, then figure out how to leave. Just head toward the Moon. I know it sounds strange, but remember where we are. This is the Fae, and what is more, the realm of the Witch of Hours. Now, toward the Moon. Always toward the Moon."

Travel through the swamp terrified Eibhlin. Between the shadows and the water's moonlight mirror play, it was impossible to tell depth. Barely any time passed before she stepped in a pool so deep she sank below the surface. She managed to scramble to shore, but her mouth tasted like slime and mud. She was also cold and wet again. After that, she found a walking stick among the rare fallen branches and used it to check for drop offs. Every now and again, a branch broke and hit the ground or splashed into the water, violating the atmosphere. Although it was crowded with trees, sound echoed in that place as though the air was fighting over it, forbidding its escape. What never changed were the taste and smell. The smell of standing water and musty air, the taste of dirt and age and rot. Like unwashed dishes. It made Eibhlin nauseous until she adapted to it. Then it only made her shudder. Her shoes had almost no purpose. When she was not wading through water, her feet sank into mud or squelched across grassy or mossy ground. She wanted to remove the chafing footwear, but she didn't trust the ground enough to expose bare skin to it.

Just follow the Moon. Ignore the shadows. Ignore the sounds and tastes and smells. Watch out for sinkholes and drop offs. Just head toward the Moon.

When the black sky began to gray, Mel called a halt. Eibhlin collapsed against a tree, her back aching and legs burning. Physically, her body heaved and shuddered, but her mind was awake. Although she knew her body needed to use the short daylight hours for sleep, she struggled to do so, spending several restless hours tossing and turning on roots and moss, staring into the twilight then back into shadows and water, till sleep finally accepted her, and she dreamed of happier days.

The second night was much like the first, a dreary march toward the unnatural full moon. However, this night Eibhlin rationed out her supplies. As of yet, she had not come upon any food or drinkable water. The forest remained as silent, dead, and indifferent as ever, like a picture instead of a real place.

By the middle of the third night, Eibhlin began to doubt. "Mel, are you sure this is the way to go? Everything looks the same."

"No, I am not," confessed Melaioni. "However, I have no other ideas of what to do. I only know this has worked before."

"Has it?"

"Unless I remember falsely."

"You've been here before?" Eibhlin asked, brushing aside some hanging moss.

"Once, though also many times. I would need to

turn back many pages of my memory to know exactly when. It has been so long. And yet this place has not changed. Stagnant as its water. More evidence of its mistress's corruption."

"Why did you come here?"

The kithara's voice dropped an octave. "Oh, Milady, please, do not make me recount that story, not here. Some other time, some other place, but not here. Although... although I suppose you do need to hear it, to hear some of it so that you might understand a little more the woman we go to see.

"The last time I came here, to this dreadful swamp, my master was a young man whose ladylove had died in an accident. He, despite knowing the warnings against it, came here to ask the Witch of Hours to send him back in time so that he might try to save his love."

Eibhlin's eyes widened. "Back in time? Can she do that?"

"Why else do you think she is called the Witch of Hours? Yes, for the price of three months of his future, she sent us back. But, alas, my master failed to save the woman he loved. And so, foolish youth that he was, he returned to the Witch and bargained away more of his time, and when he failed again, he returned yet again. And again, and again until, at last, he had no more time to sell, for those born within Time's domain cannot change the past, no matter how much they might wish to. He died in despair."

"How cruel!" cried Eibhlin. "Why didn't Arianrhod stop him?"

"Why should she?" the instrument replied. "Milady, you must remember who Arianrhod is. She is a sorceress of the black arts. It is her business. Why should she dissuade someone from the allure of her wares, even if they are false hopes? Fairies are shrewd merchants, Milady, in every sense of the word, especially those who have severed all connection to the Mortal Realm, as has the Witch of Hours, Arianrhod."

Eibhlin did not have a reply.

"Milady," said Mel, its voice a gentle thrum, "you should rest now. Dawn approaches, and I know your weariness. Do not fear. If any danger draws near, I shall wake you."

The girl nodded.

After eating a few pieces of salted meat tinged with swamp water, she folded up her cloak and laid it against a tree root. Soon, she slept, dreaming of long-lost love and days under the bright sun.

"-ady! Milady! Eibhlin, wake up!"

Eibhlin groaned. She had just been celebrating a successful harvest. The entire village had been there with food and drink. The doctor played the flute while someone else played some strings, and in the middle of the dancers spun her father and the lady with the golden hair—

"Eibhlin!"

This time, the voice was followed by a sharp pain in Eibhlin's arm. She tried to stand, but she was jerked back to the ground, as if her arm were rooted to it. She looked down. Black strings of various widths had clamped around her hand and arm and were now slithering up to her shoulder, squeezing it. She then realized they were roots. Crying out, she thrust her free hand up to the penknife on her arm and fumbled it into her grip. She stabbed down on one of the thickest roots, right where it left the ground. A terrible roar shook the air, as if a storm were crashing against the entire forest, and Eibhlin thought she could almost feel the tree beside her tremble and move. At the first creak, she sliced through the roots on her arm, snatched up her bag and Mel, and darted away like a frightened doe. Fear dulled the pain in her body, an ever-growing terror as the girl saw from the corners of her eyes the trees shift, branches bend, and leaves shake without even the slightest wind.

Swallowing a sob, she pressed on harder.

From behind her, long, spindling arms, like spider legs, clawed at her. Unstable ground made her stumble, but the trees' furious shrieks and creaks echoing in the wood spurred her onward. A few times, bits of branch caught her clothes, but no matter how thin the branches, they would not break. Most times Eibhlin could just let her clothes rip free, but when the grip was stronger, she cut it with her knife. Sap black as tar soon dripped down the small blade onto her hand and sleeve and splattered her kirtle.

The Moon watched on in silence.

Eibhlin's body wore down. Tears stung her eyes, cuts and scrapes and bruises covered her, and her breath came in painful, burning gasps.

Suddenly, sharp pain burst through her skull. The girl's head jerked back, and she fell to the ground. Looking back as well as she could, Eibhlin saw one of the inky Tensilkir, its tendrils tangling through her hair and slithering toward the rest of her. Renewed fear gave strength to her arms, and reaching back, she sliced through hair and tendrils alike. As she escaped from the harsh cries, a burning sensation ran up her arm, growing in pain till she could hardly stay standing.

Then she came to a drop off.

Due to the crowding shrubs and branches, she hadn't seen it ahead. She stumbled, dropping Mel, her knife, and her satchel and tumbled down a grassy slope. Mel and her bag slid down beside her. Finally, the ground leveled, and she rolled to a stop. For a while, she lay there in the grass. Her body ached, and her lungs could not support further flight. She waited for the trees to grab her. But nothing came.

At last, Mel spoke, its voice strained, scratchy, and out of tune, "Milady, do you still live?"

It took a minute and a few more prompts by the kithara to get her to answer. "I think so," she said.

"Oh, thank the angels and saints! I'm most sorry, Milady! The moment the sun set, they began to move. This didn't happen my last time here. I was caught off guard, and my lack of vigilance could have...."

"It's okay, Mel. Not your fault."

They both lay in silence a spell longer. Eibhlin felt comfortable for the first time in days. There was still no wind, but the air no longer felt stuffy, the ground was dry and firm, and the fresh, gentle smell of grass combined with her exhaustion lulled her near to sleep. However, just as she felt the soft promise of rest, something pricked her mind, much like at the monastery. Something didn't fit. Everything was wrong. She couldn't quite tell how, but it was. Slowly, Eibhlin propped herself up on her arm, despite her body's protests. She looked around, and her blood froze, breaking the enchantment and casting off all feeling of sleep or comfort.

The Moon stared down on a crater surrounded by thick swamp on all sides. Grass shone silver as it stood silent and undisturbed. And in the middle of it all, ringed by the only water within the crater, stood a magnificent tower bathing in the moonlight, a clock tower with a face like a miniature moon, a tower white as ivory, a tower without a shadow.

The keys shivered against Eibhlin's chest.

"Mel...."

"Yes, Milady," said the instrument. "This is exactly as I remember it. This is the tower of the Witch."

Chapter 10

Eibhlin stared at the tower.

"Maybe the trees grew restless knowing we were so close to their master's home," said Melaioni. "Or perhaps that it was taking us so long to reach it."

"How could I have missed something so huge?" Eibhlin asked.

The kithara's strings creaked with tension. "Because, Milady, this is an enchanted space. Look around the edge. Do you not see that all the trees are Tensilkir? They are forming a barrier around this place."

"So we're inside the barrier. But now what?"

"That is for you to decide, Milady."

Eibhlin looked back at the forest. A shiver ran through the trees. The trees frightened her, but the tower terrified her. But what did that matter? What did any of it matter? Had she not come here for a reason? Had she not faced that swamp, those woods, and all her previous trials for some purpose, a purpose that had led her here?

"But for what?" Eibhlin whispered.

"Did you speak, Milady?"

"No. No, it's nothing." Or so she said. Inside, Eibhlin's heart pounded. Why had she come here? Somehow, she couldn't quite remember. There was something, something about her father. No, a key? Yes. It was a key. But what—

"Milady?"

"What? Oh, yes. Well, to go back now would be pointless, wouldn't it? I can't turn back now, Mel, not after everything I've been through."

Eibhlin felt a pulsing sting in her right hand that hadn't left since she had cut the branches and her hair. She looked down. Welts and blisters covered where the tree sap had landed on her hand, and the cuff of her sleeve looked burnt. Beneath the holes in her sleeve, more stinging red spots dotted her arm. The pain throbbed up her arm, much like the time she had burned herself in her father's forge. Next, she reached up to where her hair had been. The tips crumbled to soot, and what remained of her hair was no more than chin-length, caked in mud and mire, and ragged as a cat after a rain storm. Her hair. Her hand. The scrapes and bruises. Dark elves and fae creatures and attempted kidnapping. The swamp and its clawing trees. No. Too much. She had endured too much to turn back now.

"We'll go in. We'll speak with Arianrhod," she said, the pain in her hand strengthening her will.

"Very well, Milady. I am but an instrument. I go where you take me," said Mel.

Eibhlin picked up and shouldered the kithara and her bag. She searched around till she found the iron penknife lying spotless in the grass save for some new burn marks on the bone handle. When she was sure she had everything, besides the cloak she had left behind at the tree, she turned toward the tower.

It stood like a slab of solid moonlight. Upon the clock face, neither of the hands moved; they remained forever frozen on a minute to twelve. Noon. Or perhaps midnight, the time of broken spells, a time never to come upon that tower. Just below the clock face, a walkway led from the tower down to a small gatehouse, forming a joint structure that reminded Eibhlin of a sundial. One without a shadow. A useless sundial.

There was no gate or doorway to the larger tower save the one beneath the clock face, so Eibhlin approached the gatehouse. To reach it, she had to cross the shallow stream circling the tower, water moving, she assumed, by magic. In any case, there was no choice but to cross it.

As she waded through the shin-deep moat, Mel said, "Milady, before you go farther, I need to tell you something."

Eibhlin stopped, and the moving water chilled around her legs, giving her a strong desire to hurry across the rest of the way, but she stood still. "What is it, Mel?"

"I have told you of my last visit, or series of visits, to this place and the sorrowful end to my master at that time. There is something else I think you should know.

"As soon as one knocks upon that door, no, perhaps the moment one enters this swamp, the witch's enchantments begin to work upon a person. It is an ancient, natural magic that crossing thresholds signifies crossing deeper into another's domain, placing one's self under another's power, and the deeper we go, the stronger Arianrhod's influence. This stream is one such threshold, for running water has been an especially strong boundary line since the beginning of time, and from here on, the more you cross the more you shall fall under Arianrhod's hold. For instance, there is a dreadful spell in this place that makes your reason sluggish. For another, I might become unable to speak with you. Such occurred last time I was here. Enchanted I may be, and unable to be overcome with emotions, but magic is entirely different.

"And so, I shall tell you this now, before the spells become too thick: be wary of crossing thresholds, and do not, under any circumstances, cross the threshold into the room where the Witch is. So long as you stay outside that room, a layer of the Witch's magic cannot reach you, and her control over you is weaker. Do you understand me, Eibhlin?"

"Yes, I'll try to remember," she said, though even as the words left her mouth, her currently muddy memory made her uneasy.

The kithara said, "No, no. You mustn't 'try.' This is something you simply 'must.' Now promise me you shall remember."

"Okay. I promise," she said. By now, Eibhlin's legs felt like ice as the water lashed against and around her legs, but she waited for Mel to continue.

"Good. Now one more thing, and this is another thing you must promise me. Promise me by the elven blessing upon your hands and brow, swear that you absolutely, no matter what the Witch tells you, will not attempt to change the past."

"What?" Eibhlin asked. Until Mel mentioned the idea, Eibhlin hadn't even considered it. "Why are you talking about that?"

"Eibhlin, Milady, Arianrhod is most well known as the 'Witch of Hours.' It is her greatest magic, and do not think the temptation irrelevant to you. It never is, not to humans. However, no matter what, you must not accept her offer. You are here for Mealla's key and nothing else. Do not accept anything else!"

The key! Mealla's key! That was it. That was why she had come here, to this swamp, to this tower. To find the key the Witch had obtained from the corrupt abbot. But... why did she seek the key? Why... no. Now was a time to focus. There would be chances to think about all that later.

Eibhlin promised. "Good," said Mel. "Now, touch your hand to your brow and repeat after me."

With her undamaged hand, she touched her forehead and repeated, "I swear upon Yashul's blessing that I shall not accept anything from the fairy Arianrhod, the Witch of Hours, except the key which I seek."

At last the stringed instrument seemed satisfied. It released a strumming sound resembling a sigh. "Thank you, Milady. And now, let us go see the Witch."

It took effort to move her numbed feet forward, but at last Eibhlin reached the other shore, and when she rose out of the water, the warmth immediately returned as if it had never left. More than that, her feet and clothes were perfectly dry. The tingling of her two keys sent quivers down her spine, as if they recognized magic. The feeling only increased as she approached the door.

The door was black and fashioned of wood. Silver gilded the polished surface, and it looked more like onyx than wood. Eibhlin stood before the door, hesitant. The feeling of dissonance returned and pulsed inside her head. There stood the door, and to speak with the witch, she must go through it, but need she see the witch? Could she not return... return to... she could not recall to where. But could she not go back anyway? However, the vibration of the keys sent another feeling. They knew. They could feel their sibling nearby. She couldn't back down, not when she was so close.

Eibhlin reached for the silver handle and pulled. The door didn't budge. She tried again, this time pushing. Nothing. Well, now what?

"Knock, Milady. Unless you have the key to the door, you must knock," said Mel.

Eibhlin did. The timbre was undoubtedly that of wood, and the sound echoed in the air as if in a great hall. She waited a few seconds, letting the echoes fade, and then....

"Come in."

The voice that answered tumbled into Eibhlin's mind like a cataract, wiping out all prior doubts. So sweet and cool! Like freshly melted snow on the first day of spring, or a sip of freshly drawn water on a summer's day. She wanted more! She wanted to drink from that voice!

Suddenly, a gentle pull reined in her senses. She stood just inside the entrance, her hand still upon the door handle. She could not remember opening the door and stepping through. Fear rose up in her stomach. Just two words had held so much power over her.

She would have to be more careful from now on. "Especially now that I've crossed another threshold," she muttered.

Just then, the voice came again like the sound of bells ringing clear on a winter's evening or a river's soothing speech. "Don't forget to close the door behind you."

Eibhlin did as she was told, though slowly. She could tell now, could almost taste the syrupy spells saturating the speaker's words. She now stood in a dark, circular room. It was only a single floor, and the ground and walls were bare. Light came in through small holes in the roof, giving the room an appearance as though moonlight was raining down through the black, or like stars shooting through space. Across the room stood another door.

Another threshold.

"Well, aren't you coming up?" asked the heavenly voice.

Eibhlin felt the urge to run through the door, and she only just stopped her feet as they tried to move without her will. Deliberately, she stepped toward the door, taking a deep breath as she opened it. Beyond the door stood the walkway, a walled, roofless path leading straight up to the tower. She stepped onto the pathway and back into the uninhibited moonlight.

The full Moon sat behind the tower, so that as

Eibhlin went up the path she also stepped closer and closer to the Moon. As she stared at the Moon, a sense of dread, of powerlessness washed over her. Oh, how she wished Mel would speak to her now! However, every time she tried to catch the instrument's attention, it remained silent, as though it were not enchanted at all. Up and up she climbed. Each step she felt her soul become more and more pressed within her. At last she came to the door. Eibhlin knocked.

"Come in."

By now, the pull of the voice was close to irresistible, but Eibhlin leaned into that rein on her senses, which she now imagined as a drop of sunlight resting in her chest. She opened the door, but she did not go in immediately. First, she glanced inside. Just inside the door was a short hallway, one lit in a similar manner to the gatehouse, only the beams of light were much larger, forming a patchwork pattern on the floor. At the end was another doorway.

One more door. One more threshold.

Eibhlin stepped inside. She approached the fourth door and knocked.

"Come in," the voice said again.

Eibhlin opened the door, but despite an urge so strong it felt as though it would tear her apart, she did not enter the room. She gasped.

The room was circular. Along the wall stood bookshelves packed with tomes of all sizes, most gilded with gold and gems and bearing writing Eibhlin couldn't read, as well as tables and shelves cluttered with jewels and flasks and bottles and boxes and talismans and charms. From the ceiling, on chains of braided silver several dozens of feet long, hung bells and amulets and plants and beads, all of which shimmered along with their chains in the moonlight weaving though the shadows from round windows on the walls and circular skylights in the ceiling far above her. In the center of the room, within a circle of moonlight, stood a round table, upon which sat a book and a single, shallow dish filled to the brim with water that rippled all on its own without spilling over the side. The atmosphere swirled around the room: ancient, powerful, terrifying. Eibhlin shivered.

Suddenly, the voice came again. "Didn't I say to come in?"

The voice came from directly above her, right where she knew the clock face to be, and she nearly stepped over the threshold, but the rein tugged at her soul, stronger now than ever. Eibhlin replied, "I would prefer to stay out here."

"Is that so. How sad, but very well."

Eibhlin heard the rustle of cloth, and it seemed as though the Moon herself descended before her. The figure stood tall and slender, her arms and fingers so thin and pale they seemed as though made of the moonbeams from the gatehouse. Her hair poured down in silver threads that faded to the soft violet of the Moon above, and when she moved those colors shifted and flowed like rippling water reflecting the Celestial Queen. Nearly transparent wings peaked out from beneath the hair, twitching as though with a mind of their own. Her dress was black, like the Fae sky, but rather than generate any morbid thoughts, the color seemed to bring out the glow in her complexion. The lady's face seemed like the missing face of the Moon, pale but not unhealthy, with large, dark eyes and a thin smile playing upon dainty lips.

Eibhlin felt as though she had never seen a more extraordinary woman. All memories of beauty fled in shame. All, that is, save one, a distant memory drifting through her mind like a single, small cloud in an otherwise empty sky. A warm smile and gentle touch. Someone, no, perhaps a few people? Where had she—

"Why do you ignore me, human child? Did you not come here to speak with me?"

The Witch's voice cut through the faint memories, scattering the forming faces. With flushed cheeks, Eibhlin focused back on the fairy. "So, you're the Witch of Hours, Arianrhod?"

"Would you have come here if I wasn't?" the Witch replied with laughter light as raindrops.

Drowsiness settled on Eibhlin's eyes, much like on a cloudy or rainy day, but she shook it off. She said, "I have business with you."

"Of course you do. No one visits me unless on business. I make sure of it." The fairy turned and began walking around the room, her bare feet hardly making a sound. She passed among her shelves, fiddling with one thing and then another as she spoke. "And? What might you desire? What is your wish? Do you need a curse or a blight?"

"No. I need you to—"

"Or perhaps a talisman or potion? You won't find a better sorceress in that field than I. I made sure of it."

"No. I want—"

"Or..." said the Witch, striding over to her center table and running her fingers around the rim of the bowl, "perhaps you wish to see the future? I can show you a future with absolute certainty, bind you to it even, unlike those 'provisional' prophecies of those weak elves and my fellow fae. Or perhaps a love divination? Young girls like you, always searching and hoping for romance."

"I'm not here for a love divination. I—"

"No. No, not the future. You seek a deeper, more powerful magic." Here the lady's voice sank into a tone so sweet Eibhlin could not speak. "No," whispered the Witch, drawing her finger across the water in the bowl. "No. You seek something else. Distant and ever growing farther. A distant happiness long lost. If only. If only. Echoes of days and joy and love, all gone, all lost."

At those words, Arianrhod lifted her fingers, letting the water drip back into the dish like sand in an hourglass. Then she turned and began gliding toward Eibhlin, her voice gentle, soft as snowflakes. "Yes. All lost. All gone. Such happiness you could have had, such sorrow you have endured. Looking at you, I almost weep. To think, if not for one event or one choice or one moment, you would never have had to suffer. It would never have happened; you would have been so happy. Poor child. Pitiful child. Poor, pitiful Eibhlin."

Now, the fairy stood before Eibhlin, arms outstretched as though to cup the girl's face in her hands, and Eibhlin stood frozen until that last word made her twitch. "My name," murmured Eibhlin, some of her awareness returning, her mind slowly trudging through its sluggishness as she spoke. "My name. How do you know my name?"

The fairy's hands stiffened and then drew back as she gave a slight laugh. "'How' you ask? Poor child, pitiful Eibhlin, of course I know. I know all about you. I know about the struggles you've faced in coming to me, and the dangers you've met since you left home. I know of your kind but absent father, and your anger and sadness and guilt. Oh yes, guilt. Guilt at being angry. Guilt over your jealousy for his kindness. And I know the reason for all of it. I know about the lovely woman with sun-kissed hair and warm hands and smiles. I know about the love she gave to you and your father, and the devotion and adoration he held for her. And I know the anguish he felt as he watched her slowly die. Such a dreadful illness. Yet unnamed, without known cure. Treatment after treatment. Much too expensive for a small-town blacksmith, even when the village pools its money. Too expensive. No hope. Yes, Eibhlin, poor child, I know all about you, even about that tragedy that you forgot."

All at once Eibhlin's dreams came back to her. That woman, the one upon whose lap she had sat, the one had who smiled so kindly to her, the one who had danced happily with her father, the one who had suddenly disappeared one day, leaving tears and loneliness in her place. Now that face had a name.

"Kyra. Mother."

Arianrhod smiled sadly. "Yes, 'Mother.' How your forgetfulness must make her grieve beyond the Gates, but your father never forgot. Even if he had tried, he couldn't, not when his daughter so resembles her. Every day he grieved. Poor, pitiful man. No wonder he abandoned you. To see his dead wife every time he looks upon his daughter, what else could he do?"

Eibhlin felt sorrow and anger churn in her heart. She said, "My father didn't abandon me. He just loves to help people."

"Does he now? Well surely he doesn't have to forget his daughter to remember others, does he?"

"Well... no...."

"The chicken coop. The window shutters. The leaky roof. The broken chair good only for the fire. Surely he did not need to neglect those repairs to address his neighbors'."

"No."

"Surely he didn't need to leave you alone, give all his kindness and care to others and leave you alone at night, waiting for a father who breaks his promises. Waiting for someone who doesn't come home."

"No. He didn't."

"There, you see?" said the Witch. "He abandoned you, abandoned his own flesh and blood in preference for strangers. But I can change that."

Tears slid down Eibhlin's cheeks, but she could not raise a hand to wipe them. "You can?"

The fairy witch smiled wider. "Well, not really 'me' in an exact sense, but you, Eibhlin. I can give you the chance to change it all. I can send you back, back to when your mother became sick, and you can save her, buy her the medicine and save her."

"But how can I? Where would I get the money?"

"Why, you have the means with you now, a certain purse with access to infinite wealth."

Eibhlin's fingers twitched, and a sensation tingled up her arms and pricked her mind, like a spark, a lingering thought. "I can't," she said, though to speak it was a struggle. "I can't use it. I mustn't use that purse. It's too risky."

"Risky? Surely not! Why, do you think you shall get in trouble? In trouble with whom? Is it not yours to use?"

With the fairy's words, the spark began to fade.

"And besides, even if it were not your own, surely no one would blame you for taking just a few gold coins to save a loved one's life. Such a person would be cruel, heartless."

The Witch's words wrapped around Eibhlin. She knew something was not quite right with what the fairy said... or was there? Perhaps she was right. After all, it would be cruel, would it not, to hold back when you can help another person live. Do not people deserve to live? How is it fair that some people should die just because they lack money? Why should she not just take it? Besides, it would only be a little.

"That's right. It's not fair. Only a little, just enough to make it fair. It would only be a little, and then you can live again just like before. A lifetime of happiness. A second chance. I can send you back, right here, right now. It'll only cost a little. I'll only take a little."

"A little what?" Eibhlin asked.

"Why, a little of your time, of course," said the Witch. "Time travel is not without cost. Nothing is. But don't worry. You're young, and if you succeed, why, then it won't even matter. You'll have your whole life ahead of you. It'll be like it didn't cost a thing. So? Do we have a deal? Shall I send you back? Don't you want to reclaim happiness?"

"I... I...."

Eibhlin couldn't think. The spark from before had returned and grown steadily warmer. Now it felt like a fire in her head and hands. Something also pounded in her chest, almost like some creature trying to break out from a cage too small for it. Her head buzzed. A twinge of pain jolted from her hand up her arm. Reflexively, she brought her hand to her chest, and there she felt something that seemed to hum against her pulsing hand. A flash of curiosity moved her, and she pulled out a golden chain woven from strands of hair, and on it was strung a bronze compass and a pair of keys shining like crystallized starlight.

Keys? Why did she have keys? Not ordinary, either. Magic. Magical keys... and doors... and something about the purse... and a hammer... and... and....

Lochlann's face floated into her thoughts. His smiling eyes and hearty laugh, the way he made every room warmer. Then, the expression faded. Fear, confusion, anger, grief, they were all there, though Eibhlin couldn't tell which was strongest. He was searching for something, something important he could not find. What... the hammer... yes, he was searching for the hammer. Why? What had happened to it? And why keys—

All at once, the memories spilled forth, drowning the enchantments. And all at once the drowsiness shattered like ice, and Eibhlin finally saw. Everything looked the same, the moonlight, the room, the fairy, but its wonder and beauty melted away, and deep fear and dread crashed in. She remembered the dark elf attack, the realization of evil unmasked. That sensation returned, only stronger for the mask it had worn. It was craftier, older, an ancient chaos wise in its work, and for the first time, Eibhlin saw it clearly, like a void or chasm waiting to swallow her. But only for a moment. The instant she realized it, the mask invaded her awareness once more. The glow returned, as did the sweetness of the air, and she felt her mind drifting back to sleep. But she clung to that dread as she gripped Mealla's keys. She spoke with a conviction she hung to with all her feeble strength. "No."

The Witch's smile twitched, and it seemed to lessen the strength of the spell on Eibhlin's mind, for she felt the drowsiness weaken.

"No," Eibhlin repeated. "No. I won't accept it. I'm not here to ask you for those kinds of services. I'm not here to change my past. I'm here to change my future. I'm here for Mealla's key."

"R-really? Her key? Are you sure you don't—"

"No."

"Perhaps a different time. I can't send you too close to when you sold your father's hammer. Her magic is too present then, but I can send you some time before that. You could do something to make it so you don't sell the hammer in the first place. I can make it so—"

"No! I won't use your magic. I only came for the key. Nothing else!"

All throughout her body and mind, Eibhlin felt the enchantments loosen and unravel. They didn't leave, but she felt her thoughts and emotions and senses return to her own control.

Arianrhod's smile was now clearly strained. "Only the key?"

"Nothing but Mealla's key."

At last the smile transformed into a frown. The dread Eibhlin had held onto now turned against her as fear shook her conviction, but even as the fairy's face darkened, Eibhlin did not back down. Then the fairy's face suddenly shifted again to a slight smile. Arianrhod sighed. "Oh, very well! You want the key? Well, I can't let a customer go without at least attempting to satisfy her. Bad business. Can't claim I'll grant any wish if I turn one down."

With the wave of her fingers, Mealla's key appeared in the fairy's hands, its golden-rimmed bow and crystal body shining brighter than the moonlight. Immediately, Eibhlin felt the urge to run forward and grab it, but she kept herself back behind the threshold. The Witch, as if oblivious to the battle in her potential patron's mind, waved the key slowly through the air as she spoke. "So, you want this key? Well, it'll be expensive. I procured this from a monk several years ago in exchange for one of my precious Tensilkir. A most valuable exchange. The deal was that so long as I hold this key, the tree will protect the monk's monastery from danger and draw certain types of people to it. There are a few more details, but I hope you see my point. Once I no longer own the key, that contract is void. I am rather fond of that monk, so that must be factored into the price. Are you sure you still want to purchase this key?"

"What's your price?" Eibhlin replied.

Arianrhod's smile sent shivers down Eibhlin's spine. The Witch replied, "Oh, nothing beyond your reach, but something far beyond my own. Something I cannot obtain on my own. Something of incredible value."

"Well, what is it?" Eibhlin said.

"Your hair color."

"My... hair color?"

"Indeed."

"Why would you want something like my hair color?" said Eibhlin.

Gesturing around her, the fairy answered, "It's a matter of utility, really. We fairies can take the golden color from sunbeams and use it in our magic, especially with spells like spinning gold. Not for ourselves, of course, but mortals do so desire the stuff. However, potent sunbeams are quite elusive here in the Fae. Politics and all that. Most fairies now risk the Mortal Realm for sunbeams, but my skin is far too delicate, my dear. Why, if I spent too long in the Mortal Sun, I would burn to a crisp! And so, you see, I'm in quite a bind, struggling to obtain one of the most basic ingredients for fairy magic; it's almost embarrassing. And yet, here you are, practically carrying sunbeams right in your hair. You have not even the faintest idea how much gold I could spin with the concentration you have in your hair. So that is my price: your hair color for her key."

Something in the fairy's demeanor, a certain restrained eagerness, unnerved Eibhlin. She wished more than ever that she could speak with the kithara on her back, but it seemed the enchantment had not yet weakened on the instrument.

"Why do you pause? Do you have any use for your hair color?" asked the fairy. "Have humans learned how to spin it into gold?"

"No... No, of course not."

"Then," said the Witch, holding the key to the girl's eyes, "why consider? Why hesitate? You can't even use your hair color, while I can, and you need this key. It's simply both of us trading a useless thing for a useful one. No losers, all winners. I will agree to no other offer. If you reject my price, then I keep the key, and where would that leave you? Do you really want to put everything you've suffered to waste?"

The question caused Eibhlin's breath to catch. Waste? Everything to waste? Of course not! She had to come to this dreadful place precisely because she didn't want to waste all her time and effort and pain. She couldn't let it all be meaningless. Eibhlin glared at the Witch. "Okay," she said. "You have a deal."

The radiance on the fairy's face made Eibhlin's heart sink, but there was no chance to take back her words. The fairy took a strand of Eibhlin's hair and gave it a tug. The hair fell back down, and grasped between the fairy's fingers and thumb was what appeared to be a thin thread of bright sunlight. For the next few seconds, the fairy pulled on the thread, collecting it around her fingers. And as the thread around the fairy's fingers increased, Eibhlin noticed the color disappear from the tip of what hair she could see, like the unfurling rows of a knitted shawl, leaving translucent white. When at last the fairy finished gathering the thread, she summoned a small, glass phial, removed the cap, and dropped the thread inside. As soon as it left her fingers, the thread appeared to unravel into sunlight, and the fairy quickly threw on the cap before any of the golden color could escape. The Witch smiled, and Eibhlin immediately felt sorry for whatever soul that phial's contents would be used for.

Without looking away from her new good, Arianrhod tossed the key in Eibhlin's direction, saying, "Take it. Now that our business is done, leave. If you just go out the gatehouse door, you'll exit back at the monastery, but be swift. As my contract with that monk is void, the door won't remain much longer. Oh, and another thing, be careful with your hair. It's quite absorptive right now, so the next color it touches for more than five seconds, that's the color it will be. If you're fast or lucky, maybe you can even turn it gold again. But remember, it only needs five seconds for it to change, and no second chances."

Slipping the key on her chain, Eibhlin said, "Thank you" and turned to leave. However, before she had even made it half a pace, the Witch said, "One more word of warning... Watch your step."

At once, Eibhlin recognized the magic saturating

the words, but she could not defend herself fast enough. Her feet caught upon themselves, and she tumbled to the floor. As she got back up, she cursed herself for letting her guard down, and in the middle of her self-reprimand, she thought she heard Mel's voice echo in her ears as though from far away. Before she could decipher the words, though, intense dizziness struck her, and she fell back to the floor. She felt feverish. Her body ached, and she felt nauseated. Her head throbbed as if trying to crack her skull, and her lungs felt tight.

Mel's voice came again, this time a cry of anguish.

Eibhlin lay on the floor, miserable and confused. Curling so that she could see the fairy in the other room, Eibhlin glared and tried to speak, but the aching in her head made thoughts and speech difficult.

The Witch laughed. "Child of the sun, do you blame me for your current state? I did warn you, didn't I? About your hair."

It was only then that Eibhlin realized she had fallen into a patch of moonlight, and her hair, once soft blond, now brushed against her cheek stark white.

"Still," continued the Witch, "the color isn't as pure as it should have been. Must be due to that elven blessing. Maybe it diluted the color, bleached it of some power."

"You... what did you...?" Eibhlin croaked.

"Hm? Me? Didn't I already tell you? I did nothing. Well, nothing that wasn't inevitable anyway. It probably would have changed on the walkway anyway, in that exposed light. Only now, I can actually watch you writhe a bit. Silly mortals and your 'moonstricken' state. Oh, and by the way, the deterioration of the gate is still the same. I suggest you hurry before it's unusable."

Eibhlin fumed, and the energy of her anger dulled some of the pain, but the fever and nausea would not let her charge after the fairy. It was for the best, really. If she had, she realized later, she would have crossed the last threshold and left herself completely exposed to the Witch's magic. Instead, she dragged herself to the wall and used it to prop herself up. Scraping against the wall, she made for the door to the walkway.

When she reached the door, the Witch of Hours said, "Goodbye, pitiful child. A delight doing business with you.... Still, it is a shame you cut your hair. The color really was of spectacular quality."

Eibhlin looked back to see the fairy examining the phial's shining content. Bracing herself against the door, fingers on the handle, she said in as strong a voice as she could, "You can thank your 'sentries' for that. A Tensilkir got tangled in my hair, so I cut it all off, branches and all."

The enchanted phial fell to the floor, but the sound of its collision and roll across the floor was drowned out by the Witch's shriek.

"Those idiots!" she screamed. "How could they! They know better! Traitors! Idiots! I have to hurry! The color will already be dying, could be dead. Or the sap! The tree's sap might have burned it all. No. I must hurry! How could they—"

With the sound of the fairy's screams behind her giving her some satisfaction, Eibhlin stumbled out to and down the walkway and then out the gatehouse door.

Chapter 11

Fire and screams rose into the air on the other side of the door. The clash of metal on metal and stone echoed on the mountainside. Willow-like branches hung withered or burning under the dark sky. Robed figures darted here and there as smaller forms leapt at and onto them.

Something felt familiar about this place, but to Eibhlin's fever-filled mind, it all looked alien. She could not even process enough to be afraid but only lay upon the dry earth, coughing and moaning for help. Her vision blurred; the smoke burned her nose and throat; the dry air parched her lips. A thought, distant enough to lack emotion, came into her mind.

She was going to die here. Whether by fire or sword or sickness, she was going to die.

The thought had nearly reached full consciousness when she heard a voice call from behind her, or above her; she wasn't sure. A few moments later, someone lifted her from the ground and turned her toward the sky. High above, the moon shone full from behind the worried face of a monk. He was of middle age, and on his worried brow was a sickening gash pouring blood down his face. He called out something, but between the chaos and her own head's throbbing, she couldn't make out the words. The voice behind her spoke again and struck up a conversation with the monk, of which she could only catch a few words and phrases.

Some sort of agreement was reached between the voices, for Eibhlin was soon lying across the monk's shoulder, moving away from the noise and heat. The next thing she knew, he leaned her against wonderfully cool rock in some dark place, the sounds of fighting fainter but still present. The monk tried to tell her something, but she couldn't tell what, and then he was gone.

For a few moments, or perhaps a few hours, Eibhlin swam along the shores between consciousness and darkness. Then she heard a sound like a horn and a powerful roar, like thunder mixed with terrible screams. After that, she fainted.

Her sleep was haunted by messes of people and places and she did not know what. She did not know who she was or what she was doing.

Then she saw a man, a man with a bushy beard and always smiling eyes. Except they were not smiling. They were red with grief, and dark circles and bags puffed out below them. He sat kneeling by his bed, holding the blanket to his face to muffle his sobs.

All alone. Nothing left. They had sold everything

they could, but it still had not been enough. Now it was all gone. Everything of hers was gone... except one thing. That alone he had not been able to sell. Oh, but if only he had! But he had waited too long. If only he had not hesitated! If only he had sold it! Now it was all he had. Just that one thing. The only thing left that had been hers. Only that. Only that.

The man faded back into the murky mess of dreams.

Eibhlin woke as someone picked her up. With a groan, she opened her eyes. She was in a narrow cleft of rock, sunlight shining upon the wall from around the corner. Weakly turning her head, she saw a familiar face. "Brother Callum."

The monk looked down at her with sad, concerned eyes, a bandage wrapped around his head and a small, strained smile on his lips. The look of the man reminded her of the man from her dreams, and Eibhlin's chest hurt. He said, "Good morning, and welcome back, Miss Eibhlin."

"Whe...re...."

"Hush. Don't waste your energy. You're dreadfully sick. We must give you medical attention immediately."

"S... sick?"

The voice behind her, which she now recognized as

Melaioni, answered, "The light of the Fae Moon is poisonous to those of the Mortal Realm and makes them ill, moonstricken. With continual exposure, it can even lead to death."

"Death...."

"Do not fear, Milady. Natural sunlight from the Mortal Realm weakens and eventually purges the poison, and there are other treatments that help. Although... no. No, we will speak of that later, when you are better. Till then, rest, Milady. You are in safe hands."

Eibhlin tried to nod, but the nod turned into sleep. The next week was much like her time with the elves, except less comfortable and a lot less peaceful. She lay on a cot in a medical tent, her burned hand bandaged, drifting in and out of sleep, sometimes waking for a few hours or for only a moment. On the first day, she saw a cart piled with the corpses of small, terrible creatures pass the opened tent flap. Her horror banished sleep until someone gave her a sedative. The rest of the time, she would wake to hear the sounds of shovels and solemn chanting. Always chanting. Singing the buried's departure. Every time she woke, there was always singing.

Gradually, her strength returned, but when she tried to get up, those working among the infirmary would insist she rest a bit longer. Even after a few more days, when she felt completely cured, except for the occasional throbbing in her burned hand, those caring for her would keep her in bed and give her medication to help her rest. She tried to do as they said, but after so long in bed, she was restless.

At first, she occupied her time with observation, but there wasn't much to look at. There was no decoration, only those still injured for whom there had been no room in the nearest village or whom no one dared try to transport down the mountain. She had already noticed by now that most of those assisting her and the injured were not monks but laity. There were even a few women. The assistants came regularly, but neither side could understand the other's words to the level of decent conversation. She did manage to learn, though, that Mel and Callum were away somewhere.

This last point especially irritated her, as she had something she wished to ask the kithara about. She had noticed it a few days before out of the corner of her eye when turning in bed. Her hair was not white as when in the Fae. Instead it was dark, dull, stormy gray, nearly black, the color of moonlit clouds. Or at least, most of the time. Over those days of examining her hair, she had noticed that the color actually shifted, starting out dark earlier in the day and growing lighter as the hours passed. She didn't know if the color ever returned to white, as the infirmary workers always gave her medicine when her hair had faded to about half the darkness, but Eibhlin wondered, and the long days lying awake without company bored her. So, finally, she snuck out of the tent.

Around the infirmary stood a camp. Most tents appeared to be living spaces for the monks, but there were a few laymen, too. There was little activity besides normal monastery activities, such as copying what remained of records and performing the twenty-one days of prayers and songs to mourn the dead. Most of the cleanup from the battle had been completed days ago, all the dead bodies burned or buried, so there was, thankfully, no carnage to see. The temptation to wander the camp after so long in bed pulled at Eibhlin, but then she saw one of the nurses sitting by a cooking fire, and she hurried away in the direction of the monastery itself.

The garden and well were destroyed, and the building was in shambles. Although most of the stone still stood, gaping holes were clear for all to see. One wall, where the goblins had charged through, was broken down to the ground. Almost none of the windows remained, and the roof and any other wood were charred from the fire. The stones were an empty shell, before which sat the ruins of the Tensilkir tree, the sentinel from the Witch of Hours.

Inside, the building looked much as Eibhlin assumed it would: burnt and black, with holes in the second-floor landing and rubble all over. Still, it was a change of scenery, so Eibhlin began exploring the place. She found the doorway to the cellars, the least destroyed section of the whole place, though already emptied by the townspeople and religious. An intact flight of stone stairs brought her to the second floor, and then to what likely had once been the attic, though which now just held empty space. She found the hall where she had eaten her last meal before entering the Fae. Eventually, she found what had once been the chapel. Broken stained glass windows lined the walls, and piles of blackened wood that had once been pews or benches did the same on the floor. Nothing stirred the air.

Eibhlin walked up to the steps leading to what had once been the altar and sat down facing the room. Smatterings of sunlight struck the remains of windows, casting shards of color onto the floor beside the golden glow. The air was quiet and smelled of ash, but lingering scents of incense also floated in the air.

Staring at the strong colors on the floor that resembled the shades of dusk, Eibhlin's mind turned to memories. Something about this place reminded her of the elves. It was faint, as though someone had tried to scrub it out, but it was there. It also brought to mind Vi's bell tower. No, it did not have the same fear element that quickened her soul, but it was like two notes separated by an octave, the same note just a different pitch. They somehow felt the same even if the one was cold and high and the other low and warm.

Though Eibhlin was unaware of it, she passed almost an hour in that chapel meditating on the atmosphere. She also had not noticed the time. Her own home was too far south to know that summer sunsets come late in the Northlands and to realize that, what she had thought was lunch was, in fact, dinner, a mistake nurtured by her medically-induced sleep. She did not realize how late the day really was, so she did not notice the moon's ascent until the symptoms came.

They started as just a slight chill. Then her head began to pulse with dull pain. She thought it strange, but she remained unalarmed, reasoning it was probably just a need for food and water. Deciding to ask for a more substantive meal than soup and tonic, she stood and immediately rocked on her feet as a dizzy spell overcame her. She managed to find her physical balance, but fear now shifted the scales in her mind. While she walked, the dizziness did not return, but the pulsing in her head reminded her to step with caution.

She emerged from the ruins to see the scant camp in a bustle. Another bout of vertigo struck her senses, and she had to hold onto what had once been the front threshold to keep upright. When the spell passed, she continued on toward the busy camp, her ears ringing in confusion and panic bubbling up and making her nauseated. Halfway across the distance, one of the townswomen spotted Eibhlin and gave a cry. The woman ran over, shouting something Eibhlin couldn't understand, but when the woman noticed the girl's unsteady feet, her expression transformed into worry, and she rushed to support her. By now, the headache pounded in her brain, and the sickness had Eibhlin slouching so that her hair brushed her cheeks and fell in her eyes.

White. Pure white.

Without complaint, Eibhlin allowed herself to be guided back to bed, accepted the offered cup, and let the medicine send her to sleep. She awoke with the headache gone and her hair back to slate-gray. Beside her bed sat Callum, Melaioni sitting upon his lap. The monk gave Eibhlin the same sad smile as when he had brought her to the camp. Where once had been his bandages he now bore a long scab.

"How are you feeling, miss?" he asked.

"I'm okay now but... but what happened? I was just fine and then all of a sudden I... I... and where were you, Brother Callum? You and Mel were gone for days, and I can't talk with anyone here."

Mel answered for the monk. "We were down the mountain. A path goes down into the valley, and there is a good-sized town. Abbot Callum had business to attend to, and I accompanied him in order to record the aftermath of the goblins' attack."

Eibhlin stared at the monk. "Abbot Callum?"

Callum replied, "Unofficially. To actually become the abbot, we will need to hold a formal election, but in the mean time someone needed to assume the duties of abbot, and I was chosen for the time being."

"Then Abbot Ormulf is?"

"Dead. He was among the first killed by the goblin raid," Callum explained, flatly. Eibhlin noticed he left out the customary prayer for the newly dead's repose.

Mel took over. "The night we first arrived, Ormulf did, indeed, send for the goblins, but when he went to fetch us, we had disappeared, and goblins are not very forgiving. When they learned their latest prey had escaped, they demanded the abbot's head for wasting their time. However, they could not get past the Tensilkir's barrier, so they laid siege upon the monastery. Several times, some of the monks tried to summon help with the bell tower, but the abbot, corrupt man that he was, hindered them."

"Yes," said Callum, grimacing. "He even threw some of us to the goblins to make his point. He was intent on trying to wait out the beasts."

"But then we obtained the key," said Mel. "The contract was voided, the barrier fell, and the goblins, worked into such a frenzy after a few days of bloodlust, set out to slaughter the entire monastery."

"Those of us who survived only did so because we had managed to break into the tower and call for help," concluded the monk.

Eibhlin stared at him in horror. "I... I didn't mean to put you all in so much danger," she cried. "I didn't know... I... I...."

The monk shook his head, his countenance darkening. "Don't feel guilty, Miss Eibhlin. That contract was a vile thing! And now Ormulf has met his end by his own wickedness and gone to his true masters."

"But so many innocent people died!"

Abbot Callum replied, "I know. I know, and I cannot deny my anger and sorrow. Why must so many people die for the wickedness of one, even those who resisted him till the end? I don't know. Hopefully we shall know someday, but it's quite possible we never will on this side of the Gate. But that is enough on that topic. I believe you have other questions?"

Eibhlin wasn't satisfied, but she let the matter go and instead reached up to touch her hair. She said quietly, "Mel... what's happening to me? I... I was okay and then I wasn't, and my hair is changing colors, and I don't understand at all!"

The instrument made a sound Eibhlin could only describe as a hiss. "It was a nasty trick by that Witch!

After taking your hair color, she made you fall into the moonlight, and your hair absorbed it. Here in the Mortal Realm, such a thing would be inconsequential, but the rebellious moonlight of the Fae is poisonous to those of the Mortal Realm. Before then, you were protected by such magic as Yashul's blessing countering the power of the Moon. But when your hair absorbed the moonlight, it was like being injected with it. The poison had a direct route to your mind and soul and poured in. If you had remained in the Fae but an hour more at the most, you would be dead."

Eibhlin shivered and reached for the keys hanging from her neck. "So, the moonlight poisoned me, but it's okay now, right? I feel fine."

"Did you feel fine yesterday?" Mel asked.

"W-well, yes. And the day before."

"Then it is just as I feared."

"What? What is?" Eibhlin asked.

The instrument's voice shifted into minor key. "The poison from the Fae Moon has become a part of your body. Your hair is moonstricken, tainted forever by the Fae Moon."

"What does that mean?" said Eibhlin. "I don't understand."

"It means you will never, can never, be fully cured, Milady."

Fear welled up in Eibhlin's chest, squeezing out

the air. "Y-you mean... am I going to die soon?"

"No. No, you will not die from it; at least it is unlikely," said Mel. "You mentioned your hair changing color, did you not, Milady? When we emerged back into the Mortal Realm, it was white, but right now, it is dark, dull. This is because the sunlight of the Mortal Realm, the Mortal Sun being in its proper station as ruler of the immediate heavens, counters the powers of the Fae Moon, revealing the Moon's true color without her Sun. In most cases, sunlight from the Mortal Realm would eventually purge the poison. However, because the poison is part of you, it cannot be, not entirely. Whenever the sun leaves the sky, your hair turns back to white, and the sickness returns. When we first arrived, you were sick at all hours. Now, with exposure to the sun and with the moon waning, the symptoms appear to be much weaker, which hopefully means you can live a mostly ordinary life, at least when the sun is up, and that you shall not die from the poison."

"But when night comes, I'll get sick again? And it'll never go away?"

"So it seems," said Mel. "...There is one more thing, Milady. I do not think you should travel into or through the Fae any longer."

"What?" cried Eibhlin. "But I have to! I have to use the next fairy door. I have to find Mealla. I must!"

Abbot Callum placed a hand on her shoulder. "We know," he said. "Melaioni and I have already spoken together. It didn't tell me everything, but I understand your desire to finish your journey. Only, please understand us, too, Eibhlin. In allowing you to enter into the Fae, in sending you to the Witch's house, for me I felt like I had sent you to your death. Even though you returned, you came back in this state, and Melaioni could do nothing to help you and can do nothing now.

"Now think. You have already been poisoned by the Fae Moon. If you return there, vulnerable as you are, how well will you resist her poison in the future? What if the poison simply flows into you again? What if you get pulled away from your road and so cannot find a door through which to escape? Do you understand our worry, Eibhlin? If either of us simply lets you go into the Fae again, we shall twice have done nothing but let you run toward death."

Eibhlin's heart sank. She almost cried. She wished he wouldn't speak so calmly about it. She wished he would guilt her and demand she stay. She wished he would give her something to fight, not speak to her so gently, so sadly, not plead with her with such mournful restraint.

She nearly gave in. It was true she was tired. She was scared. She didn't want to go to the Fae again. She didn't want to face any more dangers. She didn't want to be sick and helpless. She didn't want to go onward. She wanted rest, and she wanted safety. She wanted to stay. She wanted to give up, and if her memories had not resurfaced in her dreams, she might have. But now, in the back of her mind, she could hear her father's weeping. She saw her mother's smile and how he had looked at her, heard the longing and laughing voices.

Eibhlin spoke. "I... Father Abbot, when I was at her house, the Witch offered me a chance to go back in time to save my dead mother, and I refused. Even if it would have been impossible to save her, it's still a fact that I gave up on her. I threw away my only chance. I don't know how much Mel told you about me, but the reason I'm looking for Mealla is to get back the only thing my father had left of my mother's. Abbot Callum, I can't turn back now. After giving up on returning my father's greatest happiness to him, I can't also give up on the last fragment of that happiness. I can't give up. I must find Mealla!"

Callum sighed. He rose and placed the instrument on the chair facing Eibhlin. Gently placing his hand upon her head, he said, "Very well. I understand. I only ask that you wait until tomorrow. Tomorrow, our moon shall be almost half waned, and I can have the doctor mix together some medication while I gather some traveling supplies. That, at least, shall give me some comfort. Rest now, Miss Eibhlin. I shall see you off tomorrow morning."

When the monk had left, Eibhlin said, "I didn't want to make him sad."

"He already knew, as did I, that it was futile," said Mel. "But we had to try to dissuade you anyway."

"You know," said Eibhlin, "you don't need to come with me, Mel. If I die in the middle of the Fae, you'll be stuck there until someone else finds you and brings you out. And who knows how long that would be? You don't need to risk getting trapped because of me."

"No, Milady. Whether good or ill, I shall witness the end of your story. As I promised, I will not let you go alone, Eibhlin."

"Thank you, Mel," said Eibhlin. She then lay in bed, her tainted hair falling into her eyes, and a sob caught in her throat. Curling up under the covers, she began to quietly cry, and she whispered in a voice only she could hear, "Thank you."

Chapter 12

"Remember, distill one packet in water, and take it at least twice a day."

"Yes, Abbot Callum."

"Also, when your hair becomes light gray, you must find shelter. You mustn't allow yourself to be exposed when the symptoms come."

"Yes, Father Abbot."

"... I thought I said you needn't call me 'Father Abbot,'" said the monk. "I'm still officially 'Brother.'"

"But the other monks call you 'Father Abbot,'" said Eibhlin.

Callum sighed. Mel said, "You should just resign yourself to your promotion, boy."

Callum's forehead scrunched. "I never thought, at my age, that I would be called a 'boy' again."

"To me, all you humans are hatchlings. There are even some grown elves that are mere chicks to my lifetime. Respect your elders, boy."

Addressing Eibhlin, the monk asked, "Did I do something to anger Melaioni?"

She grinned. "Someone apparently called it a 'lyre' while you were in the apothecary."

"Hmph!" said Mel. "A lyre? Me? To be called such an uncouth, ignoble little instrument! Why, it is almost as bad as being called the other kind of liar! I am a kithara! A noble and elegant instrument. I have played before kings, both mortal and immortal, and witnessed the acts of great heroes. I know the epics and legends and histories of the world throughout all centuries and to all peoples. I am the Messenger of History. To be called a lyre, a mere shepherd's harp, how insulting! I do not carry such a title as alludes to deception!"

The instrument continued to fume as the three traveled through the small mountain town. Eibhlin had used the compass to find the general direction she needed and then locked it so as to travel more inconspicuously through the town. That is, if a girl with gray hair and a badly scarred hand walking with a temporary Father Abbot and carrying an enchanted instrument on her back could be inconspicuous. Still, the presence of a glowing compass might have made their passage even slower. As it was, morning had already passed, and the group had already eaten a light lunch back in town. Now, as afternoon began, Eibhlin felt the urge to continue her journey ever strengthening.

She had all three keys. All that remained was to find the next door and hope the other side of it held some clue to find the final door, the door to Mealla's home. Then she just needed to return the purse, get back the hammer, and that would be the end. All the trials, all the dangers, it was all for this last step.

Abbot Callum parted from them at the edge of town, giving them his blessing. In the forest, early afternoon sunlight played with leaf and shadow. The breeze carried birdsongs through the valley, and warmth seeped into Eibhlin's new clothes. One of the village women had hemmed up one of her own dresses for Eibhlin to replace the girl's ragged clothing. Even her shoes were different, and while they were a style new to her, she had already grown to appreciate the leather boots on account of their being more suited for hiking down mountains than her old shoes.

She wasn't wearing them now, however, as she followed a stream by wading through its shallows. When she had placed the third key into the compass and summoned the light again, it had immediately veered from the path into the woods. She soon came across the stream, saw that the needle followed it, took off the warm boots, and stepped into the cool, clear water. Mud gave way beneath her toes, and the water curled gently around her ankles. The smell of clean air, trees, and sunlight lifted her spirits.

After a while, she thought aloud, "It's so different."

"What is, Milady?"

Looking over her shoulder, she asked, "Have you cooled down?"

"No. I am absorbing sunlight that is making my surface give off its own heat waves. Now would you enlighten me as to your statement?"

"You don't have to try to be lighthearted and silly for my sake, Mel. I'm feeling fine," she said.

"I am doing no such thing. Now please tell me what is 'different'."

"You must have been trying, ever since yesterday. Even your indignation earlier, it was a bit too much. I can understand you being upset, but don't exaggerate your emotions. You are, in fact, a terrible liar," replied Eibhlin. Then, touching the burn scars discoloring her hand, she said, "As for what's different, everything is. The water, the trees, the air, everything is so different from the Witch's place. Even the grass. It smells different, as if the grass around her house was fake, made of magic rather than full of it. In fact, everything feels like that, like all the enchantments and magic were... I don't know... false, or something like that."

"That is because the magic there, the magic subservient to that Moon, is only a twisted imitation of true magic, true enchantment," responded the kithara. "But do not let yourself be fooled. It is still dangerous. Underestimating it is one of the fastest ways to be ensnared by it. It is still sorcery; it is just less true. It is less true, less natural, than even the magic in the Mortal Realm, let alone the true magic of the Fae. On that note, let me make something clear: I am not pretending to be upset. I truly feel insulted by being labeled as a lesser instrument, and for it to be a lyre, why, it is almost enough to make my strings snap. To be mistaken for that clumsy, common-place, amateurish instrument, how many millennia more will I have to stand for this?"

Eibhlin laughed as she listened to Mel's inflated indignation. It was the first time she had really laughed in many days, so the not-lyre continued its complaints for a short while longer.

Mid-afternoon had come upon them when they reached the compass's end. It was a large willow tree covered in knots, one of which hid the keyhole. With jittery fingers, Eibhlin slid the key into the lock and turned. The door opened, and she stepped through. Almost at once she arrived on the other side. No pull. No whirling or confusion of the senses, just a step forward as if through any other doorway. She arrived right by a willow much like the one she had just traveled through. All around them stood a forest much like the one before, though noticeably warmer. The day didn't seem any later, but the smells were a bit different. She knew she had traveled to some other place. However....

"Well, Milady, what shall we do? Explore? Find a settlement? Surely there is someone who—"

"This can't be happening."

"Milady?"

Eibhlin's face, which had been brimming with anticipation only a few footfalls before, paled. "No way. No way, no way! Mel, it's the same place!"

"What do you mean? I do not recall this place."

"But I do," said Eibhlin, pointing to some rocks rising beside the nearby river to form a bank overlooking the water. "Mel, this is the door the fairy used to send me to the elves. I'm right back where I started!"

"Really, Milady?"

"Yes. But... but why? The fairy said this was just an ordinary door, and she did something to connect it to Mealla's door. Why did I come here?"

"Hmm. Perhaps it is still connected and we fell through it. Or maybe Mealla's next door really is somewhere here. Milady, since we do not know, I suggest we go to the nearest town and—"

"No!" shouted Eibhlin. "No, we can't do that. The nearest town is mine, and if I go back without the hammer... Mel, I can't! Not after everything, not after turning down a chance, even a slim chance, of bringing my mother back. Mel, I just can't. Not without that hammer."

"Very well, if you insist. I cannot walk anyway, nor can I force your legs. But then, Milady, what do you suggest?" asked Mel.

"Well... oh, the compass! I've got all the keys, so now I just need the door. Since these keys open Mealla's door together, maybe I can use all three of them to... Mel, I have three keys, but there's only one keyhole in the compass."

"And the compass will only search for a single key's door at a time," said Mel. "A door that needs three keys, the compass was not made for such a case."

"So what do I do?" cried Eibhlin.

"For a start," said the instrument, "how about you sit down and have a snack. We can think while you do."

Eibhlin didn't feel hungry, but she didn't know what else to do. She sat by the river, splashing her feet in the water as the sun heated the air beyond what was comfortable. Meanwhile, she and Mel exchanged ideas.

"How about we just look around, Milady? Surely you know the area?"

"Yes, but it's too risky. I don't want to meet anyone I know. Besides, searching blindly in an area like this, it'd take too long. Oh! What if I catch a fairy like before and ask her?"

"First of all, Milady, that would be a highly discourteous, ignoble action. I am entirely against it. Second, that is a truly risky business. If you try to catch the wrong sort, well, there are stories of people who have met with quite miserable ends due to that kind of thing. Third, if you want to be out of here before anyone has a chance of running into you, we cannot dilly-dally trying to find a people who are experts at not being found. Frankly, Milady, you were quite lucky on these points last time, to run into a fairy in the daytime of so mild a nature. She must have been one of those foolish youths who spend so much time in the Mortal Realm they would rather risk humans and wing thieves than their own country."

"I know!" Eibhlin jumped up and turned toward the tree. "I'll just go back. I can ask Abbot Callum if he knows anything about the last door and-" She fell back to the ground. "I don't have a key to this door. I can't go back!"

"It was a good thought, though," said the kithara. "Really, I should have considered that before now, as the one more versed in the ways of fairies. Oh, fie to my foolishness. If only I had thought to ask the father abbot, or better yet, the elven lady. Surely at least she knows something of this business. Alas, whatever help she might have given, it is beyond our reach, for we have only before us a lock for which we have no key."

Eibhlin frowned, and her thoughts churned. Something Mel had said had spurred her mind. What was it? Lock... key... lock but no key... elves... keys... and locks, and locks and keys, and returning....

She shot up again. "Mel! Mel, maybe Lady Yashul did help us! Before we left, she said something about if we wanted to go back and... and a lock- a wrong lock? No, that's not it. Um... Something about a door and returning and keys. Mel, do you remember? You're enchanted to record that stuff, right?"

"Indeed, Milady. Only grant me a few moments. Let me see... hmmm... yes... hmm... ah! Yes. Here it is: 'Should you find the other keys and wish to return here, use all three keys on any fairy door and turn them each one full circle. They shall open the way to their doors, and you can find your way back to us.' Those are her words to the stroke."

Eibhlin's heart pounded in her chest, dulling her hearing. It seemed too great a thing to have the answer so easily found, but she couldn't hold down the hope pressing on her chest. She picked up Mel and her bag, pulled on her shoes, and returned to the tree, removing the keys' chain as she did. Singling out the first key, she said, "Are you sure she said any fairy door?"

"Upon my honor as the Messenger of History."

With hands shaking anew, Eibhlin found the keyhole and slipped in the key. She turned it. She heard a *click*, but unlike the other doors, the key did not catch, and she continued to twist the crystal key in the lock. The lock clicked three more times, on each quarter of the turn. In her hand, she felt the key shivering, and she thought she heard a quiet hum, like the fading notes of a tuning fork. Upon the fourth click, the keyhole shone. The two other keys clinked together, and as Eibhlin looked down at them hanging on the chain, their humming filled her mind. She took up the second key. Just as with the first, it turned easily within the keyhole, clicking four times. But now, the girl knew something was happening. The humming sounded nearer, clearer, sharper, like the strike of a bell. In went the third key. Quarter turn. *Click*. Half. *Click*. Three-fourths. *Click*. Full circle. *Click*.

A ring like a hammer striking glass echoed and rang in her mind. Point. Counterpoint. Eternal sound ever being reborn. When she removed the third key, the light in the keyhole burst forth, swirling and twisting and climbing across the tree till it framed the shape of decorative double doors, the tree showing behind it as though the light were an enormous, intricate window.

Eibhlin reached out and touched the light. The doors swung in, and she stepped through. On the other side was a circular room of dark blue, dark as night, with white stars swirling above her as though in a dance. The door through which she had come opened in the center of the room, a golden outline hanging in space. In the wall sat seven more doors. The first was dark, stained wood and intricately carved. The second was of simple gray stone. The third was also stone, but this one the color of sand. The fourth door Eibhlin nearly overlooked, so dark was its shade it nearly blended in with the wall. The fifth door sparkled and reflected the swirling stars across its smooth, stone face. Beside the fifth door was another one of wood, this time knotted and rough as if it were bark pulled straight from the tree. Then there was the seventh door. It was an odd little thing in that it was quite an ordinary door. It was painted a pleasant shade of green, but it had no other decoration and, when compared with its present company, was quite modest.

It was also the only door for which Eibhlin did not already know the destination. She went over and tried the knob. The door was locked. Eibhlin took her keys and repeated the process from the door of light behind her. With each completed circle, Eibhlin heard a sound like before, only this time quieter and yet clearer, as though she now stood beside the source. When she finished turning the last key, she tried the knob again. With the sound of a latch lifting, the door yielded.

What lay on the other side of the door struck Eibhlin dumb. The door opened to a wide, flat plain. Grass and flower garbed themselves in festive colors bright as spring and rich as summer. Trees stood near and far, alone and in groves, their leaves singing along with a warm wind. From one close tree hung fruit like prisms, sunlight shattering on contact into rainbows that skipped along the ground as the wind played with the branches. Nearby, a stream laughed as it ran through the grass, like a child at play. Above it all was a deep blue sky that felt as though it were so full of color it would start dripping down the sides, like too much water in too small a bucket. Through the sky, white clouds drifted lazily by, as though ignorant of the bustle and energy around them. Eibhlin even thought she saw one of them yawn, though it might have been her imagination. And streaking across the sky and filling the air, invisible unless noticed in the corner of her eye, was the rich, soft gold of the sun. But it was more than just light. In this place, it almost seemed tangible, as though it might actually kiss her.

Eibhlin tried to speak, tried to ask the kithara on her back what place this was, but her tongue wouldn't form the words. She could only quietly gasp, "Mel." And then with a light laugh. "Mel!"

"Yes, Milady," said the instrument in a voice that said that, if it could cry, it would be choking back tears. "Yes, Milady. This is true magic."

"And it is also my realm," said a voice.

There is a strangeness that comes with awe. Namely that awe is a terribly humble state. The more one's feelings move toward awe, the more complex they become till, in the purest of awe, there is a striking similarity to terror and grief and less of what one might call 'happiness'. Happiness must then transform into joy if it is to survive more than a mere moment in awe's presence.

The emotion Eibhlin experienced now was somewhere between wonder and awe. When she had met Mealla that inciting night, she now realized, she had not really met the Fairy Lady, only a fairy far from home. Here, in her home, in the realm which she was meant to occupy, the girl saw the fairy for herself. The arms of the Fairy Lady, once so dainty and fragile, now spoke of health and strength, the fingers of crafts and skill and grace far beyond the capability of the thick, stubby sticks of human hands. Her legs were like the trunks of saplings, lifting her toward the sky. Large, bright eyes shone like the morning star in the early light of dawn, and sunlight glistened off her dark hair as though it were home to astral lights. The Lady gently plucked a prism from the tree and bit into the fruit, making Eibhlin think of elves and churches and bell towers and made anything Arianrhod, the Witch of Hours, could do, any spell or incantation or curse or magic, feel like a farce.

"Mealla," she said.

"That is what your countrymen call me," replied the fairy in a voice that sent Eibhlin quivering with some unknown emotion that brought tears to her eyes.

"Lady Mealla, great Fairy Lady of Doors and Crossroads, Noble Rebel to the Moon's Rebellion," came Melaioni's voice, "My Lady Eibhlin requests an audience with you."

Eibhlin, brought out from her stupor by Mel's earthly, rustic voice, said, "Y-yes! I need to talk to you about—"

Her words died out when the fairy suddenly drew near and took the girl's scarred hand within her own. Mealla held it as though it was a baby bird, and Eibhlin more felt than saw the tinge of sadness in the fairy's face. "Take your hand and place it in the stream. Keep it there until it cools, and not a moment earlier. We can speak afterwards."

With that, the fairy let down Eibhlin's hand and watched. Eibhlin knelt beside the giggling brook. She glanced back over her shoulder, but the fairy only looked back with expectant eyes. Gingerly, Eibhlin lowered her hand beneath the water's surface. All at once, intense, burning pain shot up her arm and to the rest of her body. Reflexively, she started to yank her hand back as from a flame, but the fairy's voice cut through the pain straight to her thoughts.

"Don't remove your hand! You must keep it there until it cools!"

Gritting her teeth and fighting all instinct, Eibhlin

braced her right arm with her left and forced her burning hand deeper into the water. Time seems to slow in moments of great physical suffering, so Eibhlin couldn't know how long she endured the pain, only that she did so because any time she faltered, the Lady's voice broke through again to remind her of her task. Finally, her hand began to cool until the water felt not like fire or even a sun-heated pool but like the chill valley river from the northern mountains. Her body relaxed as the last of the feverish pain faded away, and once it was gone, she lifted out her hand. There it was, as though it had never faced hardship, without callous or scar or burn. It was a hand the likes of which could not be found even on a noble lady of a king's court. Eibhlin stared in wordless wonder.

The fairy knelt beside the girl and dipped her own slender finger into the water. In a voice that harmonized with the water's speech, the Lady said, "The sap of the Tensilkir is acidic, and the burns it causes do not heal quickly, nor often very well. However, this water heals and restores in proportion to the greatness of the injury or distortion. It must be done all at once, however, and so is very painful."

"What would have happened if I'd taken out my hand?" asked Eibhlin.

"That is hard to explain in full, but one thing is certain: your hand would have remained half-healed for the rest of your life, beyond the skill of any doctor—human, elf, or any other—to cure. Furthermore, for each injury, the water only works once, so there would be no second chances. Nor can it cure just any distortion." The Fairy Lady softly lifted a lock of Eibhlin's hair that, even in this fullness of sunlight, remained dull. "There are some things beyond this streams power, and beyond my own."

Eibhlin, too, reached up to her hair. "So I really will have this sickness the rest of my life?"

"I, too, am but a creature, human child," said the fairy. "There are ancient magics and sacred contracts I dare not try to break. But come. You wished to speak, and I shall listen. And do not think I have forgotten you, Eibhlin of the Border Town of Enbár. I knew you sought out my keys from the moment you obtained the first. What I wish to hear, and what I believe you wish to tell me, are your reasons why."

"Mealla—"

"'Lady' Mealla," whispered Mel.

"Lady Mealla," Eibhlin corrected herself. "My reasons are simple. When I sold my father's hammer to you, I didn't know it was something important to him, but it is. My mother died when I was young, and it's something that belonged to her and so is important to my father. Again, I didn't know that, but now that I do, I can't let Papa lose it on my account! I... Lady Mealla,

I want the hammer back that I traded to you. Here! I have your purse—oh! And I never used any of your treasure or anything! I promise. Now, please, I'll return this to you, so please return my father's hammer to me."

"I refuse," said the Lady without hesitation.

Eibhlin gaped. "Wha... why? I promise, I really haven't taken any of your treasure. I've barely even touched your purse. Why won't you trade it back?"

"Because I don't want that purse or my treasure as much as I want the hammer," the fairy replied. "I'm sure your musical companion has figured out why. I find it unlikely that the Messenger would miss the reason why a fairy would desire a particular enchanted hammer."

"Mel? Mel, what does she mean?"

Mel spoke slowly. "If my guess based on your description of the hammer is correct, then it is none other than that which forged the tools that carved me and, indeed, which fashioned my plating and metal: my master Chimelim's first magical item, Chimelim's Hammer by which he crafted all his remaining works. I knew my master had foolishly gambled it away after getting drunk, but I had never expected to accompany the last human hands to hold it on her quest to reclaim it. I could not be sure, however, so I did not speak of it, but now my suspicions are confirmed."

Eibhlin's eyes widened, and she stared at the fairy, speechless.

"Did I not say it was priceless?" said Mealla. "Something of that magnitude, there is little I would withhold to possess it. And as I said that night, humans have no use for it. If you were dying in a desert, would you not forsake diamonds for a cup of water? Likewise, the riches I offered were more valuable to you than the hammer, and the hammer more valuable to me. As such, even if your scale of value has changed, mine has not. I refuse to return the hammer."

"B-but I've gone through so much to get here!"

"That was your choice."

"And that hammer really is important to Papa!"

"Changed circumstances do not invalidate our previous transaction. We laid out our terms, found an agreement, and exchanged our goods. Our deal is already made."

"But it wasn't mine to make! He was so hurt, so upset! It was his last piece of my mother, of his happiness! And I stole it from him. Stole it and sold it! Please! I can't do that to him. I just can't!"

Eibhlin choked back sobs while the fairy watched her with an impassible expression. Several minutes passed. At last the Lady said, "Very well. I shall return Chimelim's Hammer."

"Then—"

"However!" the fairy said in a voice that slew the elation that had entered Eibhlin. "However, if what you say is true, then you have not only betrayed and dishonored your father, but made me an accomplice in your actions. As such, you have forfeited the right to state your terms of recompense and so must agree with my demands of compensation for not only the item you are reclaiming but also the personal injury done to me. Do you understand?"

Hearing the commanding tone, indignation sprouted in Eibhlin's chest. "Why are you doing this? After being so kind about the things I've gone through, now you're being harsh about everything!"

The fairy's voice barely changed as she spoke, but the very hardness of it shook Eibhlin's bravado. "Justice is not kind, human child. That is why humans demand mercy. Now will you accept or reject my terms? If you reject them, know that while you do rightfully own those keys, and so I cannot prevent your coming here, this is still my realm, and I can easily kick you back out."

Whether it was courage or recklessness, Eibhlin did not look away from the fairy. Steeling her own voice, she said, "What do you want?"

"A price befitting the crime," said the fairy. "You say that the hammer is a memento of your mother, a memory of her kept by your father. Therefore, by selling it against your father's wishes, you betrayed your father, indirectly your mother, and your father's memory of her. My price, then, is this: the memory of yourself as Lochlann the blacksmith's daughter."

"What?" came both Eibhlin and Mel's voices.

"Lady Mealla, you can't be serious!" cried the kithara.

"Melaioni, Protector of Understanding, Messenger of History, do your tales portray me as one who would make such a statement lightly?" said Mealla.

"But you can't—Milady Eibhlin, you can't really be considering this!" said Mel.

"I don't even understand it," said Eibhlin. "What do you mean by memory?"

"I mean," replied the fairy, "that anyone, any living being at all, who knows you as Lochlann's daughter shall forget you, shall forget the you that is his child and anything related."

"I'm still not sure I understand. And why would you even want that? What good are memories to you?" asked Eibhlin.

"Memories are a far more potent force than you may think," said the fairy. "I can find several uses for them. Now—"

"By 'anyone,' does that mean me, too? And Mel?"

"Yes, you, too, shall forget," said the Lady. "As for

Melaioni, I would not be so ignoble as to obstruct the honesty of the Messenger's records. However, it shall not be able to share such knowledge with you. Not to the day you die. Are those all your questions?"

"Yes. I think so. I accept your offer," said Eibhlin.

"Milady!" cried Mel in such a high pitch its strings nearly snapped. "Milady, please, give yourself time to consider! Think of the implications! You shall have no home, no family! You won't remember anything about them! Think of the regret!"

"Mel, I must return Papa's hammer to him," Eibhlin said. "Lady Mealla is right. I did something horrible to him. I... I sold his memory of my mother, Mel. I have to make it right! I know it sounds terrible, but I have to return the hammer, no matter what!"

Mel gave no reply.

"Are you sure of your decision? Once the deal is finalized, there will be no chance to regret or reverse your choice," said Mealla.

"Will I even remember this decision?" asked Eibhlin.

"No. You will not," said the fairy.

"Then I'm sure. Lady Mealla, I accept your price," Eibhlin said.

"Very well." The fairy lifted her hand, and the hammer appeared in a flash of light. She held the item out to Eibhlin and said, "Take it. You shall not recall the price or the reason for your quest, but you shall remember enough to complete your mission. Bring this to your father, and return it to him. The moment he takes it, the deal shall be finalized. Do you understand?"

"I do," said Eibhlin.

"Then I shall return you to the door through which you entered. May you find what you seek at your journey's end."

As the fairy spoke, light gathered around the hammer in her hand, and when the last of the words faded, the light shot out and wrapped around Eibhlin like a cocoon. Wood, water, fairy, all vanished as Eibhlin was swallowed by the light.

Chapter 13

Rain drizzled on the forest, casting everything behind a soft veil. From the ground rose a light fog, awoken by the pattering of water upon its earthy roof. Somewhere in the forest, a sparrow chirped, and doves exchanged their mournful calls, as if searching for companionship to wait out the rain. A wide river splashed nearby, welcoming its wayward, raindrop sisters to its seaward road. Just as it always did. Everything just as it always was.

Always?

How could she know that? What claim had she to that knowledge? She felt as if she had been here before, but in the same way as knowing you had seen a person in a crowd before: distant, vague, like trying to capture the curling mist. The river, the rocky bank, the tree behind her, all foggy figures from a dream.

She looked at her hands. The right almost glowed in the heaven-sent water. Her left gripped the handle of a small, silver hammer. She brought up the hammer to her eye line. Water gathered and dripped down the hammer's surface, winding around engravings of dragons and lightning. It almost seemed to hum and sing

Fairy Door 239

in her hand. This hammer... where had she....

From a chain hanging to her breast, a similar vibration and song entered her chest. She pulled up the chain. It looked braided with some form of light gold, and upon it hung a plain bronze compass and three keys of some clear stone.

Keys. A silver hammer. Keys go to keyholes. The tree....

Slowly, she pieced together the fragment. A journey. Fairies. Elves. Dark elves. Monks. Enchanted trees. Wicked magic. Poisoned moonlight. Dreary swamps. Darkness. Fear. Dread. Sorrow. All to find the keys. All to open a door. All to bring the hammer back to... to whom? She was not sure, but to someone.

All alone? No. Not quite.

"Mel?"

"Milady."

Warmth gathered in the girl's heart and spread to her chilled fingers.

"Mel," she said, "I'm back from the Fae. I did it. I got the hammer back."

"Yes, Milady. You did."

The girl's brow crinkled, though her smile remained as she looked over her shoulder at the instrument. "You don't sound happy about it. Didn't you want this to end well? Or did you want another dramatic tragedy?"

Mel did not reply.

"Mel? Mel, what's wrong?"

"I cannot say," it answered.

The girl's smile became more strained. "Well, that's odd. I thought you never ran out of things to say. Mel, really, what's wrong? You're acting strange."

"Milady, please! *I. Cannot. Say.* I truly cannot, but if you wish to understand even a little, tell me: why was it so important that you retrieve that hammer?"

"W-well... I... I suppose... I just had to, I guess," she answered, but as she did, a lump formed in her throat. "I-it doesn't really matter! The point is, I've got the hammer! Now I can return it. My journey is almost finished!"

"Then let us finish it, Milady."

With those words, she set out through the woods. However, contrary to her declaration, the kithara's request for "why" shook her and made her stomach churn and chest tighten. Why had she set out on this quest? What reason could she have? Surely there was one, right? And so, she searched and searched and searched, but all she found was emptiness.

While she trudged through the forest, the rain hardened. Earth became sticky mud, and hidden tree roots turned slick. Visibility, too, worsened as the fog answered the rain's challenge.

The taste of moist air poured into the girl's mouth with every gasping breath. Weariness clung to her body. She had just traveled the fairy roads three times without much rest and now fought against earth and heaven. But to stop now would be unwise, especially with her body and clothes already soaked through. She had to keep as warm as she could until she found shelter or else risk illness. She also did not want to be caught outside at night when she could not be sure about the strength of the moon. She had to keep going.

More than once, the girl slipped on a root or fallen stick or slippery rock, sending her to the muddy ground. Scrapes and bruises soon covered her arms and legs. One branch cut her cheek, causing warm, scarlet blood to mix with cold, summer rain. The girl shivered. But still she pressed onward, onward toward the shattered, scattered memory of whatever or whomever it was she sought.

Finally, she broke free of the trees. Hills rose before her, misty green quickly fading to gray in the fog. For a moment, her heart danced, but it soon sank again when she realized she did not know why they made her so happy. Happy enough to cry.

She wiped away hot tears, but there was no need. The rain washed away everything but the fog.

Turning aside, she walked parallel to the hills, and though she did not face them, they always remained visible in the corner of her eye: sad, gray forms hidden by fog and forgetfulness.

After a while, a house came into sight. It was a shabby structure. Dreary, isolated, and submerged in a sea of fog, beaten and broken by pounding rain, the very image of world-weary. And outside its front door, the master of the house.

When she first noticed him, she thought him a corpse. Her heart froze, and her legs lost their mobility, and she would have skirted the house if she had seen another sign of civilization or shelter anywhere. The rain showed no sign of easing up, and night could not be far in coming. Corpse or not, here was shelter, and she was beyond exhaustion. Swallowing her fear, she forced her feet forward.

It was as she neared the end of the house that the first signs of life came from the man in the form of a violent shiver and weak moan. The girl's heart jumped into her throat, and she froze again, but when her reason caught up, she rushed toward the man sitting against the doorframe. Empty flesh he seemed, clothing draping in large, wet folds over his body, arms and legs lying useless. His hair was tinged with gray, and his head hung against his chest.

The girl crouched beside the man. "Sir," she said. "Sir, are you okay?"

For a time, the man seemed not to notice her. She

repeated the question, but to no answer. Afraid she might have imagined his being alive, afraid she might have, in fact, been speaking with a dead man, the girl touched his forehead, flinching at finding it burning under her fingers despite the rain. For a moment, she thought she saw the man react to her touch, so she placed her other hand upon his arm and said, "Sir, are you alive? Can you hear me?"

With weary slowness, the man's face half-turned to her, and as with the hills and Mel's question, tears pricked the girl's eyes. All across the man's face were laugh lines, but his brow was wrinkled, and his dull eyes stared out from sunken sockets. She almost wished he were dead if only she could escape the dissonance of a dead man's face on a living one.

Glancing at the door, the girl asked, "Is this your home?"

The man gave no answer but to shiver and drop his head. A gust of wind struck them, and the man let out a shuddering gasp. Seeing she could not hope for an answer, and fearing for the man, the girl acted. She pushed open the door and, straining under the man's bulk, she dragged him inside as gently as she could and left him on a dry spot on the dusty floor. Inside, one of the windows had lost its shutters, so she ran over and fastened down the sheet that was attached to the sill. Ignoring the water leaking through the roof, she ran to the fireplace and started piling in wood. Finding the flint, she struck it till the wood defeated the moist air and wet floor and caught. As soon as the fire was strong, she pulled the man over, removed her bag and kithara, and began looking around the house.

It was as gloomy as the weather. Dust and dirt coated every surface. The table was worn, and only a single chair sat beside it. Quiet and empty and musty, as though not lived in. A twinge of sadness struck the girl's heart, but she pushed it down and got to work.

She found blankets in the bedroom trunks and wrapped them around the sick man. After she felt confident that the patient was warm, she investigated the cooking area. Most of what she found in the cabinet or hanging from the ceiling was unusable, but she scrounged together enough to make a simple soup. It was watery but sustaining.

Night came on, and the girl felt a ringing in her head that strengthened as her hair paled, but it was bearable. Though she grew feverish, she did not collapse or feel in danger of doing so. The moon must be weaker tonight, she thought as she looked at the closed shutters rattling with rain.

All night the rain did not stop, nor did the girl in tending to her patient. When she could, she cleaned the floor and table. It felt strangely natural to do so, and the hollowness in her chest soon became more painful than the pounding in her head. Once or twice she nearly cried, but she dared not leave that main room while the fevered man slept, though she wanted to. There was too much here. She did not know of what, but there was too much of it.

During the hours when morning is still night, the rain stopped and the man's fever weakened, and he woke with a groan. The girl put aside her cleaning and went over. She placed the soup on the fire again and reheated what remained of the frugal dinner. She then ladled a bowl for the man and helped prop him up. Compared to the day before, the man's eyes appeared startlingly alive, though they still remained as clouded as the sky above. It was like the difference between a thunderstorm and a spring shower, the latter less ominous even if it covers the same amount of sky. When she came over to him, the man himself almost looked frightened, but when he tried to stand, he fell to the floor, still weak from his fever.

"Don't move so much, sir," said the girl, helping him back up. "You nearly met Death just now."

"W-wh...."

"Shhh. Wait, sir. After you've eaten something, we can talk."

The man seemed mostly satisfied by this, but as she fed him, he stared at the girl with an expression she could not fully discern. Wonder? Fear? Curiosity?

Sorrow? These and others seemed alive in the man's gaze, and it made the girl uncomfortable and sad, though she could not know why.

Once the soup was gone, the girl said, "I wish I had medicine for you."

"Good lady," said the man, and her heart ached for some reason at his formality, "you've already saved me. Besides, I have a doctor friend who will visit today or tomorrow. He'll have medicine. You see I... I haven't been well recently."

The girl's eyes widened. "You've been this sick yet your friend left you alone?"

The man replied, "He did make me stay with him. I was barely eating or drinking anything, and so, when I finally fainted, my friend and his wife forced me to live with them. I don't remember much from that time, but when I got strong enough to walk again, I came back home. I... I can't remember why, but I told my friend I had to, and I did. So, my friend and his wife started coming by to check on me. It's my bad luck I got sick again and that it got bad much faster than I thought it would."

"But why? Why did you let yourself get so sick?" the girl asked, inexplicably comfortable with asking a stranger such questions.

His eyes glistened with forming tears, and the hole in the girl's heart stung. The man replied, "I... I don't know. I don't know! I think... I think it's the same reason why I wanted to be here, but I don't know. Something, I lost something precious, drove it away. Something important to me, so very important to me, but I don't remember what! I don't know! I don't... I don't...."

And the man broke down sobbing. The girl let him cry, and when he stopped, she could not help thinking he had not cried enough, but if she said such a thing, she, too, would be unable to hold back her tears.

"I'm sorry," he said. "I didn't mean to cry."

She only shook her head.

"I haven't cried since... well, I've been crying a lot more recently, but before then, I don't remember crying since my... since my wife... anyway, things have been so strange this past month or two. I've never really felt alone. All these years by myself, and I never felt alone, but then just recently... I don't know. Now I'm waiting. Always waiting, but I don't know why. It's all so strange. And what about you? Who are you? And where did you come from?"

The girl hesitated. "I... I am... my name is Eibhlin."

At her name, the man's eyes suddenly brightened, but that light soon went out again, leaving whatever remained of the girl's heart cracking. Those eyes, those lively eyes, how just that glimpse pained her! She stopped a moment more to gather herself together before continuing. "I'm a traveling minstrel. I came here to look for someone, though... though the person's name and face escape me. All I know is I need to find that person. But you, sir, you asked my name, but I don't believe you told me yours."

The man said, "You're right. I'm sorry about that. My name is Lochlann, and I'm the blacksmith for a nearby town."

The girl jumped to her feet. "Loch-You—!" Fumbling with her bag and words, she dragged out the hammer. She held it out where he could see it, and Lochlann gasped.

"That hammer! When... how... that's my wife's hammer! I thought I'd lost it! Where...."

"I found it," the girl said, trying to decide how much and what to say about her journey. "I found it in... in a fairy's possession. She sent me here to find the owner and return it. And that's you! As soon as I heard your name, I knew. No, I suppose I knew before that. I was looking for you, but I didn't know it was you. But now I can return this!"

Yes. She could return it... and then what? And why? Why did she feel the urge to give this item away? Surely there was a reason. Surely. Surely.

"Young lady?"

The girl shuddered, again caught off guard by the formality the man, Lochlann, used with her. But why should it bother her? Why did everything bother her?

She wished she could ask Mel, but the instrument had refused to speak with her since they had left the fairy door behind.

"Young lady, are you okay?" asked Lochlann.

How like him, she thought, to worry more about another than his treasure in her hands. But how did she know that? How could she assume something like that about a person she had only just met?

"It's nothing, really. Anyway, since this belongs to you, I should give this back," she said, holding out the hammer. As she did, she felt as though someone were twisting her insides.

Something was wrong.

"Are you sure you're okay?"

"Yes," the girl replied, though the twisting was now turning into foreboding. What was this? What was going on? Her voice almost rose to a shout. "Yes. Yes, I'm fine. Now just take this thing already!"

Her hands trembled. A pit formed in her stomach. Ringing echoed in her brain, and her heart quivered.

This is the end.

That thought thundered into her mind, further shaking her. The end of what? Her journey? Yes. Yes, that was true, but what else? Her ambition? Her directionless wandering? Yes. What else. Her suffering? Yes. It should be. Her searching? O-of course. Her sorrows? But what else! What else! What of the emptiness? Why did she need to return this hammer? Why had she traveled so far and so long? For what reason did she seek this hammer?

Lochlann stared a bit longer at the girl's face and then at her unsteady hands.

Why had she set out in the first place?

He reached out.

What was the point?

His eyes glanced back at her, those foggy, starless eyes. The sad eyes turning laugh lines to creases. Those eyes shadowed and tired. Those eyes without spark, without laugher, only grief.

Why was everything so wrong?

His hands touched hers. And she yanked away.

Those empty eyes now widened, as did her own. She looked down at the hammer clenched close to her chest, and then back at the confused eyes. Her mouth opened, but she closed it without speech before opening it again. Fighting the emotion building in her throat, she gasped, "I-I can't! I can't!"

"What?"

"I don't know! But... but I just can't!"

She grabbed Mel and her bag and bolted out the door, the man inside weakly calling her name after her. Water and mud splashed under her as she ran, ran back to the forest.

It was wrong! It was all wrong! Somehow, it was all

wrong! There wasn't any point!

"Wrong...," she whispered between gulping breath. "It's all wrong! That's not what I wanted. That's not—it's not what I—"

Her voice rose to a scream. "This isn't what I wanted! It's wrong! It's all wrong!"

Sobbing, she crashed through trees and brush, branches scraping and tearing, the hammer clutched close. She ran. She ran until she came across a waterway and stumbled on the loose riverbed. She fell with a splash, swallowing water through her gasping mouth. Coughing and sputtering and with blood lightly swirling away from scratches across her body, she looked up. At a bend in the river stood a familiar willow tree. Off in the east, the first beams of sunlight crept over the treetops, bathing the tree in a crown of gold and gilded emeralds. Its knotted, twisted bark became an elegant garment, and the water dripping from leaf and branch glistened like stars.

With aching limbs, the girl dragged herself out of the water. She stumbled toward the willow, wincing as she stepped on the foot she had slipped on. As she came to the base of the tree, she collapsed.

Exhaustion overpowered her. She had not slept in close to a day, and after traveling through three fairy doors, trudging through mud and forest, fighting through her moon curse, and her flight, she had not a drop of strength left. Her vision faded, and as the daybreak darkened, she whispered in her mind.

"Please... this isn't what I wanted. Please... please, I'm sorry. I'm sorry. I'm sorry."

Chapter 14

Eibhlin felt as though she had just awoken from a nightmare. Sunlight danced with leafy shadows, birds trilled their melodies, and the grass around her smelled sweet. It was like the morning among the elves after the attack, only this nightmare had been worse and so the waking all the better. With much protest from sore muscles, she sat up. At once she knew where she was, even though she had never seen this particular place before, but the colors were too bright and the smells too pleasant, and the sunlight too tangible for it to be mistakable. She was back in Mealla's realm, and in her hand she still gripped the hammer. Beside her, leaning upright against a tree, sat a kithara.

"Mel?"

"Yes, Milady."

Tears welled up in Eibhlin's eyes. She pulled Melaioni close and laid her forehead on the instrument's crossbar. "Oh, Mel!" she whimpered. "I had the most awful dream!"

"Call it not a dream, Milady," said the instrument. "Unless you propose we shared the same vision, and what a terrible one, indeed! I tried, Milady; I tried to speak with you, to tell you everything, but at any attempt, I found my voice muted, caged within me. And when I spoke to you after we got back, the weight of my sorrows so pressed upon me, I lost the will to speak. Oh, Milady, my strings shudder at the mere memory of my grief!"

"But Mel, if it wasn't a dream, why do I remember everything? Wasn't that the deal, that I would return the hammer in exchange for my memories?" she asked.

"But you never returned it. If you had, the deal would have been final, but you did not. Instead, you came back here," said Mel.

By now, Eibhlin's tears were running down the kithara's sound box. She cried a while longer before she found her voice again. "Mel, oh Mel, I couldn't do it! I couldn't return it to him! It was just... it was all wrong! He isn't supposed to be like that! Home isn't supposed to be like that! Mel, it's not supposed to be like that! I didn't want him to forget me or for me to forget him. I didn't want to give the hammer back like that. That's not what I wanted!"

"Then what did you want?" Mel asked.

Eibhlin gasped back another sob. She slowly brushed her hand over the instrument, tracing her fingers along the decorations and carvings. She felt the cool metal and warm wood. A deep, shaking sigh ran through her body.

The kithara's voice came again, deep and warm and kind.

"What do you truly want, Eibhlin?"

All restraint gave in to that gentle question, and her tears flowed freely. Between cries, Eibhlin said, "I... I want him to remember me. I want him to care about me. I want him to be my father! I want to be the daughter he loves!"

"And why can't you?"

"Because I hurt him!" said Eibhlin. "I got angry, and even if I didn't think it in that moment, I knew selling the hammer would hurt him. But I didn't know how much! I just wanted him to notice me more. I just wanted him to care about me. But I hurt him. I hurt him so much! I was wrong! Everything was wrong. What I did, what I said, it was wrong!" Eibhlin's throat hurt, and she could hardly breathe. Her voice dropped to a whisper. "I was scared. I... I had to make it right. I had to fix things so that Papa would love me again. I had to get the hammer back. But, Mel, if I have to stop being his daughter to do that... Oh, Mel! I can't! It would be pointless! I can't do it!"

"Then what will you do?" said another voice.

Eibhlin looked up. Mealla stood before her, as beautiful and powerful as before. The girl trembled and flinched when the fairy knelt beside her. However, the fairy's eyes held none of the cold hardness of their last parting, and her touch was warm and gentle as she reached up and brushed the girl's bangs from her eyes. With hands like a blanket on a cold, rainy day, she touched Eibhlin's cheek, softly wiping tears. "What will you do, Eibhlin?"

The girl's voice trembled as she said, "I will go back. I have to go back and tell Papa I was wrong, that I'm sorry. I'm so sorry!"

"He might still reject you. He might never forgive you," said Mealla.

Eibhlin's chest tightened further, but she said, "Even so, I must go back."

The fairy nodded. "Then you understand our contract is canceled. We agreed that I would take your memories, and you would receive and return the hammer. However, if you wish to leave here and still remember...."

"Yes. I know," Eibhlin said. She held out the hammer. "Lady Mealla, thank you, but I must reject your offer."

The fairy took the hammer. "Very well," she said, and Eibhlin almost thought she saw the Lady smile.

Eibhlin and Mel remained in Mealla's realm till the next morning.

"Your ankle must be treated," said the Lady. "Only that, though. Anymore, and I shall have to charge you for my services. And you can rest safely here. Tonight, you shall be under my protection. The Fae Moon's poison is also countered here; it cannot hurt you, not much. So, rest until tomorrow."

During her stay, Eibhlin ate food unlike anything she had ever known. The prism fruit dripping crystal juice, small berries that looked like pebbles or wren eggs, stalks of golden grass that tasted like sugar sticks and lemon drops and candied strawberries and several other delicacies the girl had only ever seen in caravan carts. The water was sweet, though a different kind of sweet than the grass. It was like spring and flowers and fresh air following a rainstorm.

She watched as birds flitted about and splashed around in the stream, shaking their feathers as if casting off drops of sunlight. She saw the Sun make way for the Moon with strong reds and pinks, like a young lover's blush at an innocent kiss. She saw the stars of the Fae appear. One. Then two. Then all at once, twinkling, communicating across the deep canopy. The very air felt as though it tingled with unheard speech and song. And she felt a slight pull as she watched the Moon, violet with anger, as she tried to blot out the stars and turn the heavens into empty space, but here in Mealla's realm, Eibhlin could see, even if only for a moment, beyond the veil. She wondered if any Fae outside Mealla's realm could see this. Or did they simply have to hope, never sure if they will even catch a glimpse such as this into the hidden war.

She slept that night beneath stars fighting in their rebellion against rebellion, and she slept as she had not for a very long time.

Mel woke Eibhlin at sunrise, and as the first rays shot across the expanse, she almost tried to dip her hand in them. The stars ran home to bed, and the Moon retreated until their next battle.

Mealla soon appeared and examined Eibhlin's ankle, wrapped it in a poultice, and declared it safe so long as Eibhlin didn't push it too hard in the next few days. They ate again, and then the fairy walked Eibhlin to the door.

On the way, Eibhlin asked a question that had lingered in her mind from the day before. "Lady Mealla... what would have happened if I had given back the hammer?"

"The contract would have been completed."

"Yes, but what then?"

The fairy turned to the girl, and sorrow deep as the sky above flashed through the fairy's eyes, but then it was gone, like a shooting star. She said, "Do not lose yourself to departed 'what ifs', human child. The past is gone for those of us within the Realms. And as for the possible futures, they are not for mortal eyes to see or ears to hear, not by my lips or my craft. For I am the Lady of Crossroads and Gateways, and whatever road you travel must be your choice, not mine."

Eibhlin didn't know how to respond to the fairy's words, or even if she should. Instead, she walked a bit in silence before reaching up to the chain hanging around her neck. Feeling the items hanging on the golden braid, she asked, "What do I do with these keys now?"

"Keep them," answered Mealla. "Or, if you tire of them, throw them away. They shall return to me, and I shall find them guardians once more, as I have before. For the time being, though, you paid the price for them and are now their proper owner. None can steal them, nor can they be misplaced, for unless given up freely, they always find their way back to their master."

"But doesn't that mean I can come back here whenever I want?" asked Eibhlin.

"You have paid for that privilege," said the Lady, "but I would advise against frequent visits. Humans tend to lose themselves in the Fae when in contact too much or for too long."

They came to the door. The Fairy Lady motioned as if to open it, but before she did, Eibhlin spoke again. "Lady Mealla," she said, "I-I wonder if I might make a request!"

The fairy faced the girl. "It depends upon its nature. You may at least speak it. Whether or not I accept is entirely different."

Eibhlin nodded, dug into her satchel, and pulled out the enchanted purse. Holding it up, she said, "Lady Mealla, I wanted to return this."

"I already said I would not trade back the hammer," said the fairy.

"That's not it," said Eibhlin. "I don't want to trade back. I don't even want anything for it. But I can't keep it. I can't keep something I gained by betraying my father. It wouldn't be right, and... and I don't think I could ever truly believe I was wrong if I kept it. And so, I want you to take it back."

"But then... what will you have gained from our exchange?" asked the fairy. "I cannot take back what I sold without compensation."

"It's mine to do with as I wish, isn't it? Then take it, or, if it makes you feel better, then consider it a thank you gift for all your help. I... I don't want it anymore," said Eibhlin.

The fairy frowned. Eibhlin gripped Mel's strap to stop her trembling. She wondered if the fairy had seen through her lie just now. In the end, however, the Lady took the purse, and while part of Eibhlin's mind wanted to reach out and take it back, like she had with the hammer, another, stronger part of her felt a great pressure lift. Eibhlin sighed, clasped her hands around the keys hanging over her chest, and took a long, deep breath. After exhaling, she looked up at the fairy and said, "Okay, I'm ready."

Mealla pushed open the door, and Eibhlin stepped through. She passed through the chamber of doors, through the gate of light, and there was the forest, bright and hot with high summer. Water babbled. Birds chirped. Insects buzzed. The sun felt thin compared to the Fae's, but the air and light had a different kind of beauty, a tamer beauty than the wild, overwhelming beauty of the Fae. The humble beauty of home.

Taking another breath, Eibhlin set off through the woods, just as she had two days prior. This time, however, the ground was firm, and sunlight turned the forest into a swaying canvas of light and shadow tinged with green and gold. She walked slowly, mindful of her healing foot. And of the new weight settling in her chest. Or old weight, for it was an old, familiar fear, a fear so unlike fearing dark elves or darkness or sorcerous swamps or fairy witches. In comparison, it was a quiet fear, but it was no less powerful. Slowly, step-by-step, it grew and pressed upon her heart.

When she reached the edge of the wood, she stopped, stopped on the threshold to green hills and what lay along them.

"Mel," she whispered.

"Yes, Milady," said Melaioni.

"I'm afraid. What if he rejects me? What if he sends me away? I'd rather face the Witch again than that! It's too terrifying!"

"And yet, you must move. There is no staying here, Milady. Either go forward or backward, but there is no staying. What shall it be, Milady?"

Eibhlin breathed deeply. "Forward. I must go forward, but, Mel, I'm so afraid! Please, help me."

"But of course, Eibhlin. First, take one step. Good. And now another."

And so, she made her way across the grass, a lone figure covered in mud and scratches, her gray hair tangled and messy and ragged around her chin. Step by step along the base of the hills until she saw the house. Her heart jumped when she saw it, for sitting at the front door was the unmistakable figure of her father. Her fear rekindled, stronger than ever, yet still she went toward him.

But while she was still a long way out, her father saw her and ran to meet her.

About the Author

V. A. Boston is a Catholic, the second of eight children, and a lover of language. She enjoys singing, rainy days, winter, and a cup of hot tea or cocoa by a cozy fire with a book. Her own storytelling career began with an unfinished manuscript about a knight on a mission to save a princess from a dragon written on scissor-cut paper bound with a shoelace between two pieces of cardboard. And her imagination hasn't stopped since.

Made in United States
North Haven, CT
19 September 2022